RETURN to SERENITY

OTHER BOOKS BY DIXIE LAND

Serenity

Finding Faith

Exit Wounds

Circle of Secrets

Promises to Keep

Second Chances

www.heartofdixiebooks.com

RETURN To SERENITY

Dixie Land (signature)

DIXIE LAND

Published by Alabaster Book Publishing
North Carolina

This is a work of fiction. Names, characters, places, and incidents either are the product of the author's imagination or are used fictitiously and any resemblance to actual persons, businesses, events, or locales is coincidental.

Copyright 2007 by Dixie Land
All rights reserved. Printed in the United States of America. No part of this book may be reproduced in any manner whatsoever without written permission except in the case of brief quotations embodied in critical articles and reviews.

Published by Alabaster Book Publishing
P.O. Box 401
Kernersville, North Carolina 27285

Book design by
D.L.Shaffer
Cover Concept and design by
Dixie Land and David Shaffer

First Edition

ISBN:978-0-9790949-6-5

Library of Congress Control Number: 2007902862

Dedication
To you, Mom and Dad, constant stars in my sky!

Acknowledgments
My husband, Larry, who is always there for me in my every endeavor!

My children, Brad, his wife, Diane, and three of the greatest treasures of my life, my grandsons, Ryan, Ross, and Alex.

My wonderful friend, cousin and faithful supporter, Linda.

My business partner, Dave and his lovely patient wife, Mary. My terrific writers group, a necessity in my life; Dave, Lynette, Joanne, Helen, Emogene, Kathy, John, Chuck, and new members, Caresse and Suzi.

A special thanks to Chuck, for your keen editing eye.

Dear friends, residents and co-workers at Friends Homes Guilford.

All of my loyal reader friends.

Writing pals; Ellen, Dorothy, Nancy. I enjoy our lunches!

Friend and former classmate, David R. Work, Executive Director Emeritus, North Carolina Board of Pharmacy for allowing me to consult with him and for providing information on research of lung cancer cell identification. I wish the studies' timing had been such that it could have benefited his late wife, Rebecca.

Attorney, John Barrow and his paralegal Shelly, for consulting with me on child-custody related topics.

Artist, Janice Plonski Beihoff for her beautiful painting used for the cover of ***Serenity,*** and to David Shaffer, for his wonderful creativity in adapting it for the cover of ***Return to Serenity***.

Return to Serenity

CHAPTER 1

Sunset Island Resort
Caribbean

Ross stepped up behind Maggie as she stood at the sliding glass doors gazing out at their lush, tropical surroundings. He wrapped his arms around her waist and nuzzled her neck. "Why so pensive all of a sudden, Mrs. Harrington?"

Maggie turned in her husband's arms to face him. "I'm missing Tyler. This is the first time we've been away from him overnight. And two weeks seems a very long time. Do you think he's missing us too?"

"I think he's just fine. Caroline and Charlie love him like a grandson and he's crazy about them. They'll have him spoiled beyond belief by the time we get home. And Doc and Kathryn are there. If he even has a sniffle you know Doc will be right there to check him out. And Lil will hand deliver any prescription he might need."

"I know. And I trust all of them completely. But I feel like a part of me is missing. It wasn't quite so bad those two days before we left Miami. But Ross, it really hit me as we descended over that huge sea into this tiny remote island, just how far we are from him now. He seems a world away from us."

"Mothers!" Ross tightened his arms around her and kissed her forehead. "But I understand how you feel. I miss those big blue eyes and his chubby little arms around my neck as he chatters away at me in his own special little language. And Maggie, I wouldn't want you any other way." He tilted her chin up and kissed her slowly, deeply. She melted against her husband.

The last two years had been the happiest of Maggie Thornton Harrington's life. She never would have dreamed when she fled her nursing position at an Alexandria, Virginia hospital nearly three years ago heartbroken and feeling hopeless, that she would find such happiness in the tiny North Carolina town of Serenity with a wonderful man like Ross Harrington. She thanked God every night for the dear friends she had made, for the love and joy she felt in her life now.

Soon after her arrival, when she learned she was pregnant by her former lover, her impulse had been to flee again. But circumstances had prevented it, and she was thankful for that too. The day she arrived in town, she met Ross Harrington who was recovering from heartbreak of his own. They became friends and confidants until one day they realized, that along the path to recovery, they had fallen deeply in love. When Ross asked Maggie to marry him, he told her he wanted to give her child his name and raise her baby as his own. And he had. He had adored Tyler from the moment the little boy arrived early one chilly April morning.

"Do you know what I think, honey?" Ross whispered against her ear.

"That I should unpack and decide what I'm going to wear to dinner tonight?"

"No, Maggie. I'm thinking that maybe it's time for us to start working on making a little playmate for Tyler. Then you could have two little ones to worry about when we take another trip."

She wrapped her arms around her husband's neck and gave him a long, lingering kiss. "Do you want to start before dinner or after?" she asked softly.

"What do you think?" His whispered husky words were barely audible as his lips sought hers. He pulled her even closer and Maggie was well aware of his willingness to do his part. Ross lifted her in his strong arms and carried her into their luxurious bedroom. He lowered her onto the soft satin sheets and...

...

The time raced by and soon they were beginning to think of returning home. Maggie and Caroline spoke daily to get the Tyler updates. With three days left, Maggie called to coordinate their return. Charlie would meet them at the airport and the time for their arrival had changed. She wanted to give him plenty of notice. Ross had gone down to the lobby for a moment so Maggie thought this would be a good time for the call.

Caroline answered and they chatted for a few minutes before she said, "Oh, by the way, Maggie. You got kind of a strange letter in the mail yesterday."

"What do you mean, strange?"

"It was addressed to Miss Maggie Thornton, but it had your correct home address. There was no return on it but there were three initials on the back flap of the envelope."

"Where was it postmarked?"

"Baltimore, the day before it was delivered here."

"And the initials?" Maggie asked.

"M.J.K." Caroline told her. "Do you think it could be from Michael?"

"Yes, I do, Caroline," she felt a chill run through her. "Open it now, and read it to me."

"Okay, honey." There was silence on Caroline's end of the line for a moment. Maggie heard the rattle of paper then Caroline's voice, **I am looking forward to seeing you in the not too distant future. It's signed love, Michael.**"

"Oh my Gosh! What on earth is he up to?" Maggie said angrily

Ross stepped into the room and gave her a strange look, as he stepped closer to her.

"Thanks Caroline. Ross just came back, I want to tell him. I'll talk to you in the morning."

Ross put his arms around her. "Tell me what? What is it that has you so disturbed this early in the day?" he asked with a slight chuckle.

"I am upset, Ross, and it's serious," Maggie said solemnly. It's a letter, or rather a note from Michael." She relayed what Caroline had read to her and the way the envelope was addressed.

"Is that all it said?"

"Yes. What do you think that means?"

"It may be nothing more than harassment, an attempt to upset you, at which he's been successful. It appears he's still in Baltimore." Ross shook his head. "On the other hand, who knows with Michael?"

"I don't like it. It makes me very uncomfortable," Maggie said. "Perhaps we should go home early. Maybe Tyler's in danger."

"Honey, he'd have no way of knowing we're away and that Tyler is with the Kellers. No. It sounds to me like it's you he's interested in. He addressed it to you, with your maiden name. He's clearly not acknowledging our marriage."

They continued to discuss Michael at length. Ross promised Maggie that he'd try to have Michael checked out when they returned from vacation.

Then the conversation returned to Tyler and the Kellers and how well he was doing in their absence.

"See," Ross said, "he's been just fine like I knew he would be."

"Caroline says he asks about us everyday. She told me they have a big sheet of paper with fourteen boxes on it posted on their refrigerator. Everyday he scribbles in one of the boxes with a red marker. When he has them all colored, mommy and daddy will come home. She says he loves doing it. It's the first thing he heads for every morning while she's fixing his breakfast. So precious!" Maggie smiled as she pictured him doing it.

...

With two days left Ross asked, "How would you like to spend your next to the last day here?"

"I think out on the beach."

"What? No shopping today?"

"I think I'm shopped out, and I have gifts for everyone. No, let's just be beach bums today."

"That's my kind of day," he said, heading back toward the bedroom to dress for the day. I'll go change and we can get some breakfast downstairs and then head out to the surf and sand."

"I'm going to call Caroline, and then I'll be right with you."

Ross went into the bedroom while Maggie reached for the phone and dialed. There was no answer. She left a message saying she'd try again later. Perhaps Caroline was tending to Tyler and couldn't get to the phone.

Thirty minutes later they were dressed and ready for a lazy day in the sun. Ross headed for the door. "Let me try Caroline again before we leave." She started for the phone but it rang before she reached it. "I'll bet that's her now."

Ross stepped closer as Maggie lifted the receiver. "Oh Hi, I thought it might be you. I tried you earlier and..." Her smile turned to a frown as she listened.

CHAPTER 2

"When did it start?" Maggie asked. She listened…"You did the right thing. What does Doc think?"

Ross was at Maggie's side instantly. "What's wrong?" he asked, a frown suddenly creasing his forehead.

"Hold a minute, Caroline." Maggie covered the speaker on the phone. "It's Tyler. He slept so late this morning that Caroline went in to check on him. His face was flushed and when she laid her hand on his forehead, he was burning up. She put him in a tepid bath and gave him some liquid Tylenol, but it didn't seem to make a difference. She and Charlie took him to Doc's. They're there now."

Ross shook his head. "Was he sick yesterday?"

"Caroline says he was fine."

She returned to her phone conversation. "Is Doc handy? I'd like to talk to him."… "Okay. We'll wait here for his call."

Maggie was on the verge of tears when she hung up with Caroline. Ross wrapped his arms protectively around her and pulled her to him. "He's with Doc now. They did the right thing to try to bring the fever down and then got him straight over to Doc."

"I want to go home. Call the airport and see if we can get a flight out today."

"I agree. I'll use my cell phone to keep this line open for Doc." Ross reached for the phone book that lay on top of the desk, fumbled until he found the number and dialed. As Ross's conversation continued his tone became exasperated.

The resort phone rang. Maggie picked up before it could ring a second time. "Thank God, Doc. How is he?" As she listened, her face clouded. She bit her upper lip as tears filled her eyes. "I hear Caroline crying in the background. Is there something you aren't telling me, Doc?"

Ross flipped his cell phone off and didn't wait for Maggie to finish her conversation with Doc. He bounded out of their room and took the elevator to the lobby. He reached the desk clerk who was browsing through a newspaper. "We have to fly out of here today!" Ross began. "Please let me see your list of checkouts."

"I'm sorry sir," the clerk began. "I can't show you that."

"Look, I'm not trying to be difficult. I have a child who is very sick back in the States. My wife and I **have** to leave today. I'll pay someone, anyone double to give up their seats, and I'll pay for them to stay the extra days. Please, just let me know who's leaving!"

The clerk studied Ross's face for a moment, then pulled out the drawer and laid some forms on the counter. He stepped away from them and appeared to busy himself a few steps away. "As I said, I can't show them to you, but I guess I can't keep you from looking at them."

Ross copied down the names and room numbers. "Thanks," he laid a fifty on the counter as he left. "I appreciate it." Now he had to convince one of the couples to give up their seats.

...

Maggie said good-bye to Doc and hurried to the door to look for Ross. There was no sign of him. Not good, she thought. He must be having trouble making reservations. She paced as she waited. *First that note and now this.* She was on the verge of tears again. She glanced at her watch. It had been ten minutes since she and Doc hung up, it seemed more like an hour to her.

Finally the door opened and Ross stepped in. He looked solemn. He was short of breath.

"Ross? Were you able to get us on the plane?"

CHAPTER 3

"I was. The only flight out today leaves in two hours. We fly into Miami and on to Raleigh. We'll rent a car to drive home."

"Oh, Thank God! But we'll be driving to the hospital."

"What did Doc tell you?"

"He's sending Tyler to the hospital in Fayetteville. His fever is still terribly high. He wants them to do some blood work. They're taking him by ambulance. Caroline's a nervous wreck, she's so upset and blaming herself. She and Charlie will follow in their car and stay with him until we get there. Doc thought he was dehydrated so he started an IV to get some fluids back into him quickly. He said Tyler's very lethargic, probably from the high temp and whatever's causing it." Her voice broke. "I wish we hadn't come," she said through sobs.

"Honey," Ross said, as he reached out to hold her. He'd have had the fever whether we were here or there. He's in good hands, and we'll be home tonight."

Ross looked at his watch.

Maggie said, "We need to hurry if we're going to make the flight."

"I've already checked us out," Ross said.

They went into the bedroom together and began packing.

Two hours later, they headed out of paradise and into problems.

Dixie Land

...

It was after 10:00 p.m. when their US Air flight landed in Raleigh. Maggie went to the car rental desk while Ross picked up their luggage. As soon as they were headed for Serenity, Maggie phoned Doc Miller's home. Kathryn answered, and Doc's voice came on the line a moment later.

"How is he? Did they admit him? Is his temperature down?" She listened.

"I'm so relieved…I'm glad they did…we're going straight there. Thanks, Doc. We'll see you soon." Maggie ended the call.

Maggie was visibly relieved as she relayed Doc's message to her husband. "His fever has broken, they're waiting for the lab results and they're keeping him overnight for observation. His temp got up to 105. They want to make sure it's going to stay down. If he's doing alright tomorrow, they'll probably discharge him. Doc said the last time he checked Tyler was still in the ER, but they were expecting to transfer him to a room in pediatrics soon.

...

An hour and forty-five minutes later Ross and Maggie pulled up to the emergency entrance of the Cape Fern Valley Hospital in Fayetteville, North Carolina.

"I'll go in and see if by any chance he's still here", Maggie said. If not, they can tell me how to get to Pediatrics."

"There's a parking place. I'll go in with you." Ross pulled forward and turned into one of several empty parking spaces. They got out and walked the few steps to the entrance.

The department appeared quiet for the moment. A triage nurse was seated at a desk a few steps from them. She smiled as Ross and Maggie reached her. Maggie introduced herself and inquired about Tyler. The woman reached for a log book before saying, "I remember him. They moved him to pediatrics soon after I came on duty tonight. He was doing much better, his fever had broken. He's such a little doll baby and he was so good." She ran her finger down the page. "Here it is, he's in room 5560. If you'll go down that corridor," she said pointing to her left, "you'll find a directory of the hospital on the wall beside the elevators."

"Thanks," Maggie said, feeling relieved. "Do you know if the couple who brought him in is still with him?"

"They were when he left here," the nurse said. "They were so worried about him, typical grandparents."

Maggie didn't correct her. As far as she was concerned, Caroline and Charlie were his grandparents.

"I should probably move the car," Ross said heading back toward the door they had entered. "I'll meet you in his room."

Maggie thanked the nurse again and started down the hallway. As she walked, she glanced down the aisle to her right. In the distance a tall, well-built, dark-haired man in green scrubs stepped out through the curtain around one cubicle and disappeared through some double doors.

Maggie froze in her tracks. A chill ran down her spine. Her heart pounded. "Oh dear God!" escaped her lips.

CHAPTER 4

Maggie turned back toward the triage desk. There was no one there. She wanted to ask someone the name of the man she had just seen, but she didn't see a soul in the ER now. Still feeling shaken, she continued on toward the elevators. She checked the directory then rode to the fifth floor.

When she got off, she followed the signs to pediatrics. Once inside those double doors, she walked the short distance to the nursing station.

The woman in white sitting at the desk looked up from her chart. "May I help you?"

"Yes. I'm Mrs. Harrington. My son, Tyler, was admitted to your unit earlier this evening."

"I thought that's who you were. His grandparents described you. They said you'd be arriving late. He's in the last room on the right at the end of the corridor to your left. He was asleep when I checked on him a few minutes ago. His temperature is down to 100 degrees. He's doing much better."

"Thank God," Maggie said. "May I go down now?"

"Certainly."

Maggie started down the hall but stopped after she had taken a few steps and turned back. "My husband should be arriving any minute. He went to park the car."

"That's fine. I'll let him know where your son is."

As Maggie continued on her way, she thought perhaps she should have asked about the man she saw in the ER. But quite possibly the nurse here wouldn't be able to help her. Better to ask someone in the department.

She reached Tyler's room, knocked very lightly then pushed the door open.

Caroline jumped to her feet and ran to greet Maggie with a hug. "I'm so glad to see you. I feel just awful about this. We've been so careful with him, given him our complete attention," her eyes were becoming teary.

"Caroline, these things happen. I certainly don't hold you responsible in any way. I'm just thankful you got him right to Doc and that he's doing better. Ross is re-parking the car."

Maggie embraced Charlie then stepped over to Tyler's bedside. As if he sensed her presence, the toddler rolled onto his back and pulled himself into a sitting position rubbing his eyes before opening them wide. "Mommy!" He squealed.

Maggie reached down and lifted him into her arms. She covered him with kisses, mingled with her own tears. "Mommy's here, precious. Mommy's home. I love you sooo much!"

He wrapped his plump little arms around his mother's neck and kissed her cheek. "Mommy rock?"

Maggie glanced about the room and saw a rocking chair in the far corner. "Yes. Mommy rock," she told him as she kissed his cheek again. It had been their nightly routine ever since he was born. She would rock him each evening with Ross sitting on the sofa, and she would sing him a lullaby. Then they would both carry him up the stairs to his room. If he hadn't already fallen asleep, he did soon after he was placed in his crib. It was Maggie and Ross's favorite time of day.

Ross stepped into the room as they began to rock.

"Daddy! Daddy!" He reached his arms up to Ross.

Dixie Land

Ross lifted him from Maggie and kissed him. Then Tyler turned back toward his mother and leaned down as he reached out to her.

While he snuggled into his mother's arms again, Ross greeted Caroline and Charlie.

Very soon, Tyler drifted off to sleep. Maggie continued to hold him for a while longer, loving the feel of his soft smooth skin and relaxed little body in her arms. How she had missed this precious little soul.

After she lifted him into his crib and covered him with his own downy blanket Caroline had brought from home, she joined the others on the opposite side of the room.

"As I was leaving the ER, I saw someone...I saw Michael. I'm terribly upset!"

"Honey, it couldn't be." Ross said. "There was no one there but the nurse when I left you. He'd have no way of knowing that Tyler was going to get sick and be admitted here today." He kissed her forehead. "You're tired and upset over all of this and that's perfectly understandable."

"It was him, I tell you. I was headed toward the elevators and, for some reason, I glanced down one of the ER corridors. A man in scrubs stepped out of one cubicle and disappeared through some doors. I only saw him for a few seconds, but I swear to God it was Michael!"

"Honey," Caroline began. "I think that note upset you and then this with Tyler on top of it. I almost didn't mention the letter until you came home but then I thought I should. Maggie," she continued, "I think Ross is right. You're tired, and I know you're worried about Tyler. Sometimes our minds play tricks on us. No one who looked anything like Michael has had anything to do with Tyler the whole time we've been here. And, we've been with him every minute since he arrived."

Ross reached for Maggie's hand. "I'll go down to the ER and talk to the nurse if it'll make you feel better."

"I think Caroline's right, little girl," Charlie added. "What would he be doing down in Fayetteville? That letter came from Baltimore just a couple days ago."

Maggie sighed wearily. "I certainly hope you're all right. But, I swear, he looked so much like Michael that it gave me chills!" She turned to Ross. "I would feel better if you'd go see what you can learn."

...

Ross returned some fifteen minutes later. "The nurse said no one who fits Michael's description worked in the ER. She described the doctors who had been there this evening. None of them sounded anything like Michael. They ran from rotund, middle-aged and balding, to young, blond and bearded. She thought possibly you could have seen someone from the lab or some other department. I agree with Charlie. I don't know what Michael would be doing in Fayetteville. There's nothing here for him. He seems to need the bright lights of a big city. Besides, with a history like his, I doubt any hospital would hire him. I can't believe he didn't lose his license."

"Me either. He probably knew somebody in the right place," Charlie added.

"Thanks for checking, Ross." Maggie sighed. "You're both probably right."

But inwardly, Maggie wasn't as convinced as the rest of them were. She wasn't sure why Michael would be here either, but then she wasn't sure why Michael had done a lot of the things he had in the past after their break-up. And because of their history, she feared what he might do in the future. She had been very frightened when she learned he'd hired a private investigator to watch her after she broke off with him, left Alexandria and settled in Serenity. It was shortly after that she realized she was pregnant.

Only her closest confidants knew Michael was Tyler's biological father, and Maggie had been adamant about keeping the secret. She learned that Michael desperately wanted, and needed, the insurance money she received as settlement from the plane crash that killed her father and sister. Later, one of her friends who knew the truth, in an attempt to help protect Maggie from Michael, was unwittingly tricked into revealing that he was responsible for Maggie's pregnancy. And, after Michael learned that, he became obsessed with reuniting with her. It would be the perfect way for him to get his hands on her money and pay the substantial back-taxes he owed for his unreported gambling winnings. Later, his addictions brought heavy losses. He had gone so far as to show up at their wedding, wielding a gun, in an attempt to stop the marriage and get her back.

He hadn't contacted them since their wedding day when he was led away from the ceremony in handcuffs, but he was never far from Maggie's thoughts. He had maintained a low-profile after he made a deal with the IRS by agreeing to undergo treatment for his addictions and working out a payment plan. They had even heard, through their friend Lil's nephew, Kevin Williams that he had been released from rehab and then had a relapse and had readmitted himself. Even though he had gone voluntarily, Maggie still considered him very unstable. And so, she had continued to keep her guard up. She felt extremely protective of Tyler when it came to Michael even with distance between them.

"Maggie? Did you hear what I said?" Caroline touched Maggie's arm lightly.

Maggie returned her attention to her companions, "I'm sorry. No. I didn't."

"Now that you two are here, Charlie and I'll go home." They stood. "Maybe you and Ross can get a little rest in these chairs. Call us in the morning, and let us know how he is." With that, Maggie and Caroline embraced, and the Kellers left the room.

Return to Serenity

As Maggie nestled into the chair her thoughts returned to the vision of the man she'd seen in the ER. A chill shot through her. She knew what she saw. He did look like Michael. Again, a terrible uneasiness crept over her; it was going to be a long night.

CHAPTER 5

When Maggie finally slept, it was a very light sleep. What had her mother called it when she was little, "sleeping with one eye open?"

The minute the door to Tyler's room opened at 6:00 a.m., Maggie was wide awake. The night nurse checked Tyler's temperature.

"Good. It seems to be staying down. It's 99.6."

"That's wonderful," Maggie said.

"We have a pot of coffee in the break room. Would you like me to bring a couple of cups in for you and your husband?"

"That sounds good." Maggie glanced at Ross; he was still sleeping. "Just one cup for now, thanks."

The nurse left the room and returned soon after with coffee, cream and sugar for Maggie. After being aroused to have his temperature taken, Tyler was wide awake. He sat up in the crib and reached up for his mother to hold him. Maggie lifted him into her arms and they sat in the rocker.

Before long, Tyler's chattering woke Ross. He pulled his chair closer to them and Maggie shared her coffee with her husband.

"I wonder what time they'll decide to release him today. With his temp staying down, I can't imagine they won't," Maggie said. "Hospitals are notorious for not keeping anyone in for long."

At eight o'clock the day nurse knocked on the door. "We've just had a call from the lab. Something happened to yesterday's specimen and they want to draw another."

"No!" Maggie's response was immediate and adamant. Ross looked at her in surprise.

"I'm sorry, Mrs. Harrington," the nurse said. "It won't take long. They'll send someone to the room. These things happen occasionally."

The thought of Michael was foremost in her mind. "No. His temperature has stayed down, and I want to take him home now. If our doctor in Serenity feels he needs blood work, he'll draw it."

"He hasn't been released yet. The pediatrician who saw him yesterday doesn't usually come until after nine."

...

Ross was able to persuade Maggie to wait for the doctor to check Tyler over and release him. She didn't feel herself start to relax until they left the Fayetteville city limits and headed down the highway toward Serenity. Tyler fell asleep in his car seat soon after the trip began.

"Honey, I've never seen you as uptight as you've been over this."

"I know, Ross. I can't help this gut feeling I have. All I wanted was to get Tyler away from that place. When that mess-up happened with the lab, and I thought of the man I saw last night, I…"

"Honey, I wish I could say something to put your mind at ease. I know you're tired. I think you'll feel better once we get home and everyone gets a good night's rest."

"I hope so," Maggie said softly. But, right now, she wasn't at all sure that would make a difference.

When they reached town, Ross drove straight to the clinic. While they were waiting to be seen, Maggie used her cell phone to call Caroline and let her know they were back. Doc's wife,

Kathryn, and her sister Mildred, the receptionist, visited with them through their office window.

A short while later, Lindsay Payne, Maggie's replacement opened the door to the waiting room and called Tyler's name. As they reached her, she grinned as she gave Maggie and Tyler a big hug before leading the way to the examining room. "I sure missed you while you were away. And I'm relieved to see this little guy doing so much better today," she said animatedly. Her pager buzzed. "The doctor calls. I'll be back in a minute and get his temp." With that she closed the examining room door, and Maggie and Ross began the wait. Tyler quickly squirmed off Maggie's lap and went over to the toy basket in the far corner of the room.

"That's a good sign," she said, smiling as she watched him. She turned back to Ross. "Lindsay looks good, doesn't she?"

Ross nodded. "Has she been dieting again? What is it this week?"

"She's been on a cottage cheese and boiled egg diet the last few weeks. Lindsay was blond and as tall as Maggie's five-foot-seven inches. Unlike Maggie, she was constantly dieting, trying to get down to a size twelve dress. It was an ongoing struggle.

Lindsay loved to cook and desserts were her specialty. The nights she didn't cook for herself, she ate with Caroline and Charlie. And in the last month, she had started to date a man from out of town.

When she moved to Serenity, she took the apartment over the Keller's garage which had been empty since Maggie and Ross were married. Lindsay and the Keller's daughter, Joy, had been best friends during nursing school, and she had often spent the weekend in Serenity with Joy since she was from Montana and got home only once a year. She had fallen in love with the little town and its people. Lindsay was devastated when Joy and her fiancé were killed in an auto accident late one Friday night on their way to Serenity. But for a mix-up in the work schedule, she would have been with them. This had made it even more difficult for her to deal with the tragedy.

After graduation, Lindsay stayed in Chapel Hill to work at the University hospital. A couple years later she fell in love and hoped to be married the following summer. When the relationship ended badly, she went to Serenity to visit Caroline and Charlie for a few days. She had always found comfort in spending time with them. When Joy was alive, they had been her substitute parents.

While there, she learned there was an opening in the clinic. Maggie was on maternity leave and didn't really want to go back full time. Lindsay had met Doc years earlier during a visit to the Keller's. Joy and her doctor fiancé planned to return to Serenity after graduation allowing Doc to semi-retire. Lindsay had even discussed the possibility of joining them.

During her visit with the Kellers, Lindsay interviewed for the position and moved to Serenity two weeks later. Maggie returned long enough to orient her to the job. They connected instantly and became close friends immediately.

Recently, there was a new man in Lindsay's life, Tom Cullen. He was some sort of government contractor with a high security clearance. He lived midway between Serenity and Sanford and traveled out of there.

He and Lindsay had met quite by accident. One Saturday afternoon after leaving Maggie and Ross's home, Lindsay had a flat tire. He was driving behind her. And when he saw her tire blow, he stopped to change it for her. They had visited for a few minutes after he finished, and he asked her to dinner on the weekend. Since, she'd become very taken with him. Maggie and Ross were eager to meet her Tom.

Maggie broke the silence. "When Lindsay comes back, I'm going to invite her and her friend for dinner next weekend if that's okay with you."

"Fine with me. I look forward to meeting this 'Mr. Wonderful' of hers."

"For her sake, I hope he really is. She was so hurt by the last man she put her trust in."

There was a brisk knock on the door and Doc stepped in. "Come here, little fellow and let me have a look at you." Doc stretched his arms out toward the child.

Tyler stopped what he was doing and toddled over to Doc with a big grin on his chubby little face. Doc stooped down and lifted him up over his head before sitting him gently on the examining table. Tyler squealed and a belly laugh rolled out of him.

"Won't be able to do that much longer," Doc said. He winced, then placed his hand on the small of his back.

After a thorough going over, Doc pronounced him fit and let him choose a treat from his goodie basket. "Just keep an eye on him; I know you will. I'm not sure what brought it on but he seems to be doing fine now. I would like to draw some blood since they had a foul up at the hospital."

...

A short while later, the Harringtons stepped out of the clinic and started toward their car. "Hey, wait a minute." Maggie turned back to see Lindsay in the doorway. "Let's meet for lunch soon. I want to hear all about your vacation on that gorgeous island!"

"We will. I was going to call you anyway. Ross and I want you and Tom to come for dinner on Saturday. We're dying to meet him."

"Sounds good. We had dinner plans for that night anyway. We can have it with you! I'll bring a dessert," she said. "I've been a good girl for two weeks and I'm getting sick of cottage cheese!"

Ross strapped Tyler into his seat while Maggie got in and rolled her window down. "I'll call you tomorrow and we'll set a time."

...

That night when Maggie slept, she dreamed a horrible dream. Her shrill screams woke Ross. When he shook her to wake her, she had tears rolling down her cheeks. She couldn't bring herself to tell Ross what she had dreamed. And she couldn't stop trembling even when he gathered her in his arms and held her close.

CHAPTER 6

Tyler seemed to have recovered one-hundred-percent from his episode of two days ago. The lab report on the blood Doc drew was normal. Maggie busied herself unpacking and catching up on laundry. That was the only downer connected with a trip, getting everything washed and put away again.

Caroline came by in the late morning. "Charlie made arrangements with Ross to get the rental car back. I thought I'd visit with you while they take care of that."

"I'm glad you came by. I just put Tyler down for a nap. He's full of himself today."

"I'm so glad. He had me worried sick."

"Little ones can get sick in a hurry and they seem to get over it about as fast. Come with me," Maggie said, "I was just headed to the laundry room to put another load in."

Caroline followed her down the hall. Maggie pulled a chair away from the wall. Have a seat here while I fold these clothes," she said stepping over to a table on one side of the room.

"I'll help," Caroline said as she reached for a pile of Ross's socks.

"I want you and Charlie to join us for dinner on Saturday. We've invited Lindsay and Tom too. Have you met him yet?"

"No. And we'd like to. They always meet somewhere when they go out. Charlie and I would like to check him out, if you know what I mean."

Maggie chuckled. "You're such a mother hen," she said. "But I feel the same. She wouldn't let anyone into to her life for quite a while after the breakup and now she seems to have fallen pretty hard for this guy. I just hope he's as nice as she thinks he is."

...

The week flew by, and Saturday dawned sunny and warm. Maggie decided to bake a ham and make potato salad, baked beans, and homemade rolls for dinner. Since it was so lovely, they'd eat outside in the gazebo Ross had built for her the past spring. Maggie found herself looking forward to a relaxed, fun evening with good friends. She invited Lil to join them, but she'd had to decline saying that her nephew Kevin had called and asked her out to dinner. There was a new lady in his life, and he was bringing her to meet his aunt.

Maggie was glad Lil and Kevin were growing closer again. It had taken some time and a real effort on Kevin's part, but slowly he had convinced his aunt that he was truly repentant for the harm his friendship with Michael Kerns had caused them all. He appeared to have broken all ties with Michael. At the thought of Michael Maggie's stomach churned. She must do something to put her mind at ease about him. And she must do it soon; she didn't like living this way, feeling fearful so much of the time.

She finished mixing the potato salad, covered the large Tupperware container with an airtight lid and put it in the refrigerator. Her phone rang, startling her for an instant. She closed the fridge door and lifted the receiver.

"Hello...Oh hi, Lindsay." She listened for a moment. "I'm so sorry. Of course we want you to come anyway. I'm just disappointed that we won't get to meet Tom. Thanks for letting me know. See you at 7:00."

Dixie Land

Maggie hung up and dialed Ross at the drugstore. Lil answered and told her Ross was tied up on another call.

"That's okay. You can just give him a message for me. Tell him Lindsay called and said that Tom can't make it tonight. He's been called away on business…I know, that's a bummer on a Saturday, but I guess that's the government. Anyway, I'm disappointed. We were all looking forward to meeting him." They talked for a few more minutes. Before they said goodbye, Maggie said, "Call me tomorrow and tell me all about Kevin's special lady." Lil promised she would.

Maggie went upstairs to check on Tyler. He was sleeping peacefully with his cuddly toy baby lion wrapped in his arms. It was his favorite toy, this week. She smiled as she blew a kiss across the room then turned and went back downstairs.

She went to the telephone and dialed information. When the recording came on she spoke clearly, Cape Fern Hospital, Fayetteville, NC. When she received the number, she jotted it down and broke the connection. She lifted the phone again and dialed. When the call was answered she asked for the personnel department.

A woman answered and asked to put her on hold for a moment. Maggie's stomach churned as she waited. Finally, the lady returned.

"I'm trying to reach a…a relative who is employed there. It's extremely important; his name is Michael Kerns. I believe he works in the lab."

CHAPTER 7

The woman hesitated briefly before saying, "I'm sorry, Ma'am. We aren't allowed to give out that information."

"But it's urgent that I reach him," Maggie pleaded.

"I'm sorry. Between hospital policy and the federal HIPPA privacy rules, there isn't much we can tell anyone anymore. I'm sure you understand." The woman abruptly broke the connection.

Maggie hung up and talked to herself. "You didn't really expect to find out anything from them did you?" Before she could move on to plan two, she heard Tyler calling to her. "That's it for now," she said as she headed up to get him.

...

The dinner was fun despite the fact that Tom couldn't make it. After Charlie and Caroline left and Tyler was tucked into bed, Ross, Maggie and Lindsay went out to sit on the porch.

"I'm so disappointed that they picked today of all days to call Tom away" Lindsay said. "He was looking forward to meeting all of you. He'd been expecting the call any day though. He told me that when I invited him."

"Where did he have to go?" Ross asked.

"He couldn't tell me. I do know it's out of the country."

"Wow," Maggie said. "You're dating a spy!"

Lindsay laughed. "No. Not now, anyway. He's an international business consultant. He used to be with the CIA. So, perhaps he was a spy at one time."

Dixie Land

"Do you think he's still with them? That this 'consultant' is just a cover?" Maggie asked.

"No, I really don't. He said when he worked for the CIA he lived in the D.C. area. He was married. His wife wasn't happy because he was away so much of the time. He resigned to please her, and they moved down here because she wanted to be closer to her family. He said that wasn't the answer for them either and they divorced. There weren't any children and it wasn't a bitter divorce. He said they had just grown apart. He went into the consulting business. He told me he was considering a move back to the Washington area before we met. I sure hope he doesn't."

"For your sake, I hope so too." Maggie said. "Do you know how long he'll be away on this assignment?"

"No. He said he'd call me when he could but I doubt he'll be able to tell me much about where he is and when he'll be back."

"Maybe we can get together when he gets back," Ross added.

After the sun set and the evening began to chill down, Lindsay said she needed to leave. They agreed to meet in church the next morning.

Maggie yawned and stretched. Ross reached for her hand, brought it to his lips and kissed it. "A great evening, honey, and dinner was delicious as usual."

"It did taste good; you know how I love ham. And Lindsay's chocolate, coconut, pecan pie was pure ambrosia."

Maggie snuggled against her husband and Ross wrapped an arm around her shoulders. They sat quietly for a few minutes.

Finally Maggie broke the silence. "I made a call to the hospital in Fayetteville this afternoon."

"Oh? Why did you do that? Something to do with Tyler?"

"No. Michael."

Ross turned in the swing to face Maggie. "Honey, are you still upset about what you thought you saw in the ER?"

"I know what I saw, Ross. And the botched specimen just…"

"Maggie," Ross interrupted. "You were worried sick, and you were tired. I think the lab was very careless, but it's happened before. It's a believable mistake though careless. People aren't perfect. And there was absolutely no threat to Tyler at any time during his stay. When Caroline and Charlie weren't with him, you and I were."

"I know," Maggie said reluctantly.

"You know how much I love Tyler, Honey. He couldn't be any more mine if he were part of me. And, God knows I'd do anything on earth to protect him if I thought there was any danger to him. We haven't heard or seen anything of, or from Michael since our wedding day. I feel like you're obsessing on this. I just don't like what this is doing to you." He pulled her to him and kissed her.

She returned his kiss and when he released her, she spoke softly, "Perhaps you're right." Maggie let it drop for the evening. And she made up her mind not to talk about it any further for now. But she wasn't about to dismiss what she saw until she did some more checking.

CHAPTER 8

Lindsay was sick on Monday, and Kathryn called Maggie to see if she would fill in. Caroline and Maggie had an agreement that she would watch Tyler whenever Maggie had to work, so Maggie went in early and Ross dropped the toddler off at the Keller's on his way to the pharmacy. It was a busy day and Maggie didn't get off until after 6:00. Ross and Tyler were at home and Ross had a roast in the oven when she came in. "You're an absolute blessing!" She declared. "What would I do without you?"

Tyler heard her voice and ran to her with arms outstretched. She lifted him up and planted kisses on his cheeks and neck.

"Well, you're about to find out for the next three days."

"Oh…my…gosh! That's right. How could I forget? You're leaving for the convention in the morning, aren't you?"

"Yep. I'm off to the windy city. And Maggie, I hate to have to leave you when I know you're feeling uneasy about Michael. If I weren't one of the speakers, I'd cancel. But I'm committed. If I can leave early, I will."

"Don't worry about me, dear. I'll be fine. I have Caroline and Charlie, Lil, Lindsay and a whole lot of others to look out for me."

"Why don't you go to town and stay with them until I get back, or better yet, have them come out and stay with you?"

"I'll be fine here alone, Ross. I am feeling better about things. If anything makes me the least bit uncomfortable I'll ask them to come out."

"I've asked Sheriff Barton to put a patrol out here while I'm away."

Maggie smiled at her husband and nodded. "Thanks, we'll be fine," she said. "Do you want to drive to the airport and use the long-term-parking or shall I take you?"

Charlie offered, and I took him up on it. He loves to feel involved; it's been great for them both. Being grandparents certainly agrees with them and they're a Godsend for us. You and Tyler can sleep in, unless Lindsay's still under the weather."

"No. She says she's much better. She plans to work tomorrow. I'm going up to change. I'll throw some clothes in a suitcase for you while I'm there."

"I've already packed. Just change and come back down. I'll have a glass of wine waiting for you."

...

Maggie got up with Ross at 7:00 a.m. and they ate breakfast. After Charlie picked him up she went back to bed until Tyler woke up at 8:30. While she was feeding him, Caroline called. She asked to take him to a story hour at the library later in the morning. "You want to come along, Maggie?"

"Thanks, but I think I'll take advantage of the time to get a few things done around here. Yesterday was kind of a lost day on the home front. Do you want me to bring him to town?"

"If you're gonna do that you might as well go with us. No, I'll come for him. Maybe we'll stop and get a little lunch and some ice cream before I bring him home."

After Caroline and Tyler left for town, Maggie went to her dresser drawer where she kept her old address book from when she lived in Alexandria.

When she lifted it from the drawer, several photos slid out of the back inner flap. She reached down to pick them up.

They were of Robyn and some of the other nurses she had worked with in Virginia. The last picture she picked up was of Michael and her. She shook her head. It made her even more determined to learn as much about his whereabouts now as she could. She started to rip it up but changed her mind and slid it behind the flap in back of the others

She found Robyn's page in the address book. "I hope this is still a good number for you," she said aloud. She went into the kitchen and over to her desk and lifted the phone receiver. She wavered for only a moment then quickly dialed the long distance number lest she get cold feet. She would find the right words when Robyn answered. After all, her former friend had done her a favor by warning her about Michel's obsession with her and the fact that he had lied to her about Robyn being pregnant.

The phone rang four times before the answering machine picked up. "Hi. This is Robyn. Can't talk right now. Leave your number, and I'll get back to you." She heard a beep.

Maggie cleared her throat. "Hi, Robyn. It's Maggie Thornton Harrington…I'm probably the last person you expected to hear from, but I need to talk to you. Would you please call me when it's convenient? You can call collect." Maggie left her number before she hung up.

She hoped that Robyn would return the call and that it would be before Ross returned. She didn't want him to know she was still pursuing her strong feeling that she had seen Michael and that he was a threat to Tyler.

...

Maggie read that night until she felt her concentration abandon her. It was a luxury she seldom had these days, reading in bed. When she turned the bedside table lamp off, she drifted off to sleep within minutes. She was startled when the shrill chirp of her phone awakened her. She reached for the receiver. It was Ross. She propped her pillows behind her head and didn't bother to turn the light on. "So how has your day been? ... Really? ... Then I bet you're tired. I have to admit I am...but I'd just fallen asleep. ... Okay. I'll talk to you tomorrow evening. I love you, too." They said goodbye.

Maggie glanced at the lighted dial on her clock. It was only 9:30. She must have been tired. She thought for a minute of reading again but decided against it. She rolled onto her side and was dozing off when the phone rang again. Perhaps Ross had forgotten to tell her something. She reached for the speaker button and said "hello."

"Maggie? It's Robyn. I hope I haven't called too late." Her tone was distant, cool.

"No. I wasn't asleep. And thanks for calling back." Maggie propped herself up on her elbow and tried to sound friendlier than Robyn did.

"I **was** surprised to have a message from you. What do you need?"

"I need some information. I need you to tell me everything you know about where Michael is now and what he's doing."

There was silence on Robyn's end of the line.

CHAPTER 9

"Robyn? Are you still there?"

"Yes. I'm trying to figure out why you care about what Michael's doing."

"It's important. Do you know anything about him?" Maggie said

"Not really," Robyn said haltingly. "I don't know anything about his whereabouts these days. The last I heard was a few months ago. Why? Surely you don't want him back."

"Of course not! What did you hear then?"

"Well you know he went into rehab after he got into trouble with the IRS and caused problems at your wedding. You are still married, aren't you?"

"Yes. Very happily. It's just that I got a note from Michael a couple of weeks ago and then I thought I saw him around here recently. That made me nervous and very curious as to where he's living now."

"I doubt it was Michael unless you were up this way. After he got out of rehab the first time they took him back on staff at the hospital, but it didn't last more than a few months. He got to gambling again and started not showing up at the hospital. They let him go and he went back into rehab up in Baltimore. My guess is he's still around that area. I haven't heard any word of him since. He and I didn't exactly part the best of friends, you know." Robyn's tone had warmed a bit since they began talking.

"Thanks. I was very tired at the time, but I really thought it looked like Michael. They chatted for a few more minutes. Then Maggie thanked Robyn again for warning her in the past and for the information she had given her tonight. They agreed to talk once in a while in the future. *Perhaps a good thing to come out of this*, Maggie thought.

Maggie reflected on their conversation before she went back to sleep. Ross, Caroline and Charlie, and now Robyn, all of them very doubtful - everyone was probably right. It was just someone who resembled Michael a lot. He wouldn't have any reason to move to Fayetteville and very likely they were right, he'd never leave the proximity of Atlantic City. Gambling, and all that went along with it, seemed to be a disease with him. It seemed to be in his mind and blood. It was a shame, too. He was such an intelligent man, and he had a natural charm about him. He came across as a very caring doctor with his patients. *What a waste*, she thought as she drifted into sleep.

...

Maggie woke from a jumbled dream at the crack of dawn the next morning. She was at the hospital in Fayetteville looking for Michael. It seemed so real that she sat up and looked around the room to check her surroundings. She shook her head, glad to be in her own room, in her own bed.

She lay for a few minutes unable to fall back to sleep. *Why not?* She thought. *Why not ask Caroline to watch Tyler and I'll drive to Fayetteville and check out the lab for myself?* She justified her plan by telling herself that the dream might be an omen. She rose, dressed, then went downstairs and fixed breakfast. She called Caroline and made arrangements without telling her where she was going. Shortly after, Tyler woke and called her. They ate, and she drove him to the Kellers' then headed for Fayetteville.

She parked in the parking deck and went into the hospital. After checking the directory, she found the lab. She lingered in the hall for a short while and watched the comings and goings.

Several technicians came out with metal baskets filled with color-coded tubing, tourniquets and syringes.

There were two entrances to the lab so she wandered between both. One of the technicians who was returning to the lab stopped and ask, "Can I help you find something, Miss?"

"No. But thank you. I'm supposed to meet someone here. He should be along any minute."

The woman nodded and went into the lab.

Maggie spotted a chair a short distance down the hall and decided to go sit down. She still had a good view of both lab doors. She picked up a brochure, opened it and looked between the reading material and the lab entrances. Thirty minutes later, she glanced at her watch. An hour-and-a-half had passed since she arrived.

As she began to chide herself for her foolish venture, the far lab door opened and a tall, dark-haired man stepped through it and headed in the opposite direction from where she was sitting. "Michael!" She said under her breath as her heart began to pound. She bounded out of her chair and hurried down the corridor after him. He was walking quite fast. She was jogging and still not gaining on him.

In desperation she called out, "Michael."

He didn't appear to have heard her. He didn't turn around but continued on.

"Michael, wait! I need to talk to you!" She was running now. He was waiting at the elevator with his back to her not acknowledging her at all.

The elevator door opened as she reached him. She put her hand out and touched his shoulder as he started to step through the doors. "Michael, please." She sounded breathless. "I need to talk to you."

He turned to face her and looked down into her eyes. "I'm sorry, Miss. Were you speaking to me? I thought you were calling to someone else. I'm not Michael. My name is Ward."

Maggie was speechless as she peered up at him. Though from his build, carriage and coloring she would have sworn he was Michael. When she looked into his face, he didn't look much like him. She felt embarrassed.

"I'm sorry. My mistake. I...I thought you were someone else. It's just that from a distance..."

"No problem." He said with a smile. "I'm sorry I wasn't. Obviously you wanted to see him very much." He laughed. "No harm done." A woman was holding the elevator for him. He started to step in.

"Wait, please. May I talk to you for a minute, Ward?"

He turned back to her and waved the elevator on. "Sure. What can I do for you?"

"Have you worked in the lab here for long?"

"For a couple years, why?"

"Is there a man named Michael Kerns working in the lab?"

"No."

"Is there any man in the lab who resembles you? Or in any other department?"

"No. Not that I know of."

"Do you always work the day shift?"

"I usually do, but I also take call. The weeks I'm on call, I come in at night. Why do you ask?"

"It's important that I know. Could you have been on call the second week of August? I know this seems strange but..." Maggie became silent as she watched him remove a small organizer from his pants pocket and open it.

"As a matter of fact, I was. You're good," he said with a smile.

"You've been a great help," Maggie said. "Thanks for talking to me."

Ward pressed the button for the elevator and Maggie turned and headed for the exit doors. Ross and the Kellers had been right. She must have been worried and exhausted and she had mistaken this man for Michael. Today she understood what an easy mistake it had been. She felt a little foolish, but she also felt relief. Michael hadn't been there after all, and the lab had simply made a careless mistake.

...

The night Ross returned, Maggie prepared his favorite meal, prime rib, mashed potatoes, frozen baby lima beans, homemade yeast rolls, topped off with lemon meringue pie. She had missed him and Tyler had too, especially for their bedtime ritual. After the meal, all three went up to Tyler's room to rock.

Lindsay had several days where she felt a little ill. She called Maggie each morning to say that she was going to go in to the clinic but to alert Maggie that she may have to leave early. Each time she started feeling better after she got to work.

Life quickly settled back into their normal routine with Ross taking Wednesday's off now that he had Ryan full time in the pharmacy. They also alternated work weekends. Ross still took call for emergencies, something unheard of in larger cities but a perk of living in a very small town where all of the townsfolk were friends.

A short while after the Harringtons returned from their vacation, Reverend Townlee called Maggie and asked her to come by the rectory on Tuesday afternoon. He said he had an idea he'd like to discuss with her. He sounded very excited.

...

While Maggie met with the preacher and his wife, Ross and Lil were busy in the pharmacy. The phone had been ringing constantly all day long.

"For two cents I'd just let it ring," Lil said, as she again reached for the receiver.

Ross shook his head and chuckled. "You're too curious to do that," he said as he heard her say 'hello.'

"Could I tell him whose calling please?" She listened. "Oh. Please hold a minute," she said coolly. Lil put her palm over the speaker and turned back to Ross. Her expression was troubled.

CHAPTER 10

Maggie left the Townlee's home and decided to stop by the clinic for a few minutes. It was nearing closing time, and she hoped Lindsay could talk for a few minutes. She'd even offer her a ride home as Lindsay often walked to the clinic as part of her new fitness program. They hadn't seen one another since the night of the dinner party, though they had spoken on the phone almost daily.

"Hi, Maggie. It's good to see you!" Kathryn Miller said.

"How has your day been?"

"Not too bad. I think we're actually going to get finished on time tonight. Doc's with our last patient of the day now."

"Is Lindsay handy?"

"I'll see," Kathryn said. She picked up the phone and pushed a button.

A few seconds later, Lindsay stepped into the office. "Maggie! I'm glad you stopped by. I was going to call you tonight."

"I was in town for a meeting and just finished up. I thought I'd drop in for a few minutes and give Tyler and Caroline a little more time together before I pick him up. Will you be ready to leave soon?"

"Yes. Can you give me five minutes?"

"Sure. Did you walk or drive today?"

"I walked." She spun in a circle with her arms outstretched. "I think it's helping."

"You're looking good. You can ride with me if you want. It's up to you."

"I will. My legs are tired this afternoon. I'll be right back," Lindsay said. She stepped back through the door to the examining rooms.

...

Maggie unlocked the car doors and she and Lindsay got in. "I'm so excited! I couldn't wait to tell you," Lindsay began. I called the house but got your answering machine. Maggie glanced at her friend as she started the car. Lindsay's cheeks were flushed, and her voice exuded enthusiasm.

"Don't keep me in suspense. What is it?"

"It's Tom! He called from Virginia. He wants me to come up for the weekend! He said he's missed me and wants to see me. Oh, Maggie, I think I'm falling in love with him. And I think he really cares about me, too."

"That's wonderful. I hope you have a great weekend. Do you know when he'll be finished with this project he's on?"

"He isn't sure. It's ongoing. That's why he wants me to come up there for a few days. He wanted me to come Thursday evening, but I told him I couldn't do that."

Maggie pulled into the Keller's driveway and parked. "Do you want to go in with me and visit for a few minutes?"

"I wish I could, but I need to decide what I'm taking with me this weekend and then do some laundry."

She and Lindsay parted and Maggie headed for the Keller's back door. Caroline and Tyler opened the door as Maggie lifted her hand to ring the bell. After hugs and kisses were exchanged, the women visited for a few minutes before Maggie and Tyler left for home.

When they arrived, Ross was starting up the porch steps. He waved and headed for Maggie's car. He opened the back door and unstrapped Tyler's seat belt and lifted him into his arms. He leaned down and kissed Maggie as she came around the car.

After dinner was finished and Tyler's evening ritual had been completed, Ross said. "I need to talk to you about something, honey."

"Good. I need to talk to you, too."

He said, "You first."

"Remember I told you the other day, Reverend Townlee called and said he and Marion had an idea they'd like to run by me and a request? Well, I went to talk with them this afternoon. Marion wants to start a morning nursery/play school at the church for a couple of hours each weekday. They believe we have a number of families in the church with young children whose mother's would be interested. They'd sing, play, color, be read to, you know, the things little ones like to do."

"That sounds great," Ross said. "Did Donald and Marion just want your opinion?"

Maggie chuckled. "How well you know this little town. They wanted my opinion…and my help."

"Why doesn't that surprise me?"

"They're going to ask Liz Harper and Judy Farrell to help out also. Marion thinks they will and, that way, we can work out our schedules on a weekly basis. Of course, Marion would be there everyday. You know how wonderful she is with little ones."

"If you want to do it, I think it's a great idea. And if the others agree, it sounds like it'll be a flexible schedule for everyone."

"Then I'll do it. I thought you'd feel that way. Now, what did you want to talk about?"

Ross shifted on the sofa to face her. "Melanie called me at the pharmacy today. She asked if she could come and talk to both of us on Saturday. She said it was urgent."

"Did you ask her what it's about?"

"I did. She said it was something she could only talk to us about in person."

What did Ross's ex-wife need to see them both about? Maggie couldn't help but feel a little uneasy. Several times in the past when she had contacted Ross, it had meant problems for them.

...

Try as she might, throughout the week Maggie's thoughts kept returning to Melanie and their Saturday meeting. True, Melanie hadn't contacted them in a while, but Maggie couldn't forget how hard she had tried to win Ross back.

Maggie was convinced that if Melanie could have forgone the HLA testing for Keri's paternity, and allowed Ross to think her little girl, Keri, was his, she definitely would have. Now, as Maggie's concerns about Michael had diminished somewhat, she had another worry to replace it. Melanie. What was she up to now?

She was careful not to mention anything to Ross to lead him to believe that she felt anxious about this upcoming meeting. She knew without any doubt that Ross was devoted to her and to Tyler. She didn't want him to think she was paranoid, but she had to admit to herself, that for the first time since their marriage, she was. And she knew it was all her own doing.

Finally, Saturday arrived. Melanie planned be at their home around 2:00 p.m. Ross and Maggie had decided it would be best to take Tyler over to be with Caroline and Charlie. Because they weren't quite sure what to expect from Melanie's visit, they didn't want to chance any unpleasantness or a scene of any kind.

At one o'clock, Maggie drove to Serenity. She and Tyler knocked on the Keller's door. Charlie answered almost before Maggie removed her hand from the knocker.

"I've been watching for you, little lady," he said grinning.

"I know which one of us you were really watching for," Maggie said with a chuckle.

Charlie laughed too as he reached out to the little boy. Tyler grabbed his hand and off the two went into the living room.

Caroline stepped forward, "I'll tell you one thing for certain, Charlie's convinced there's no little boy on earth like that precious little one of yours. You, Ross and Tyler are the most wonderful blessings in our lives."

"And you are in ours. I don't know what we'd do without the two of you."

"Maggie, I know you're concerned about this meeting with Melanie. Please don't be. I can't imagine anything on earth she could do that would create problems between you and Ross."

"Thanks, Caroline. You know me so well. I know you're right. I don't know why I've let things bother me as I have recently. I'm way too young to be going through menopause."

They both laughed at that. Maggie leaned down and kissed Caroline's cheek. "We'll see you later. And thanks."

Caroline waved at Maggie as she pulled out of the driveway and headed for home. Traffic was light this Saturday and she arrived home with ten minutes to spare before Melanie's expected arrival.

Ross and Maggie sat in the living room with CNN on, each lost in thought and both oblivious to what the newscaster was saying. Maggie glanced at her watch. "It's 2:15. Do you think she's forgotten she asked to see us?"

"No telling with Mel," Ross said. "Let's give her a few more minutes. Chapel Hill traffic could have slowed her down. Today is a game day, you know."

Maggie picked up the latest issue of Southern Living from the coffee table and began to leaf through it. The doorbell broke the silence.

"I'll get it," Ross said rising from the sofa."

Maggie rose and followed him to the door. The bell sounded again before they reached the front door. "I'm coming," Ross called out. He unlocked the dead bolt, turned the knob and pulled the door open. He stared into the face of his ex-wife. He instantly wondered why she was alone - why she hadn't brought Keri with her?

All three were silent for a moment as their eyes met.

Maggie spoke first. "Melanie! What's wrong?"

CHAPTER 11

"Could we please talk here on the porch?"

"Yes, certainly. What's this about?" Ross asked.

"I hate that I have to call on you, but I don't know where else to turn," Melanie began. Her once vibrant blue eyes looked lifeless and tired; her blond hair once lustrous looked dull and was considerably thinner than Maggie remembered. Maggie opened the door wider. "Are you sure you wouldn't rather come inside?"

Melanie looked back toward her car. Ross and Maggie's eyes followed hers.

"Keri's in the car. She fell asleep a little while before we reached Serenity. I'm glad she did, because this gives us a few minutes to speak privately. Do you mind if we just sit here on the porch so I can keep an eye on her?"

"Not at all," Maggie said. She and Ross stepped outside. Melanie sat down in one of the chairs, Maggie and Ross took seats on the swing. They were silent as they waited for Melanie to begin.

Melanie fidgeted in her seat then cleared her throat. "I guess you can tell by looking at me that I'm not well." She paused for a moment before continuing. She coughed and cleared her throat.

"What is it, Mel? What's wrong?" Ross asked.

Melanie's eyes moistened as she began again. "I have the big "C", to be exact, I have lung cancer." She struggled trying not to sound so melancholy. She forced a faint smile as she said, "Isn't that a bummer?" Her voice broke, and she coughed again. "I'm sorry. You'll have to forgive me, I'm very emotional today."

"Oh, Melanie! I'm so sorry. How awful for you."

Ross looked stunned. "My God, What a blow! How long have you known?"

"A few months ago. I had a cough I couldn't get rid of. When I went to have it checked out…" her voice faded.

"Why didn't you come to us before this?" Ross asked.

Maggie reached out to her. "What can we do to help you?" Suddenly, Ross's ex-wife held no threat at all for her. She felt only sympathy for this woman with a child to raise by herself and a deadly disease to cope with in addition.

Melanie stared into Ross's gray-blue eyes as she started to speak again. "The reason I asked to talk to you both is that I've started chemo-therapy, my second round. Thank God, today's one of my better days. But, most of the time, I'm so sick. It's dragging me down even more than I expected. I want to leave Keri with you and Maggie, Ross. Please. She looked from one to the other.

Neither Ross nor Maggie spoke for the moment as Melanie's revelation and her request sank in.

"Just until the worst of this is over," Melanie continued. "Until I can take proper care of her again. She's so little and needs so much attention… and, right now," she wiped away a tear that escaped her eye, "I can't give it to her. I can't even go to work most days. Some days I can barely drag myself out of bed. I've applied for disability, but it won't kick in for a while. I can pay you. I have some money saved… I'll give you money for her food and anything else she needs."

Ross searched for words. "I wouldn't even consider that. You know we wouldn't take money from you. Mel, I.…"

Dixie Land

"Wait, before you give me your answer, there's one other thing I have to tell you. I told you when we met at the park that day a couple years ago that I'd never deceive you again. You've been kinder than I ever deserved, and I'm so grateful to you, Ross…and to you, Maggie. I feel I owe you this. Then you and Maggie can make your decision."

Maggie reached for Ross's hand and held it tightly.

CHAPTER 12

"Okay, Mel. Tell us," Ross said quietly.

"This is embarrassing for me," she said casting her eyes down. After a slight pause she continued. "Keri is…she's Michael's daughter. After you went for the testing and we found out she wasn't yours, Steve, the man I left you for was tested. He wasn't responsible either. Though we partied as a group and Kevin was there too, I was never intimate with him. No, by process of elimination, I know that Michael Kerns is Keri's father. And I know you can understand why I don't have any desire for him to be involved in her life."

Maggie felt a pang of acid shoot through in her stomach, but she showed no emotion. *Michael certainly did get around*, went through her mind. *Sex seemed to be another of his addictions.*

Melanie continued looking from Ross to Maggie. "I have friends, but they're all single, without children, and they couldn't give her what she needs like you and Maggie can. And there's no way on earth that I'd turn to Michael. I know what a tremendous favor I'm asking of you both. I wouldn't come to you if I wasn't desperate for Keri's sake. But I honestly believe you both truly love children. I love Keri so very deeply. She's the best thing I've ever done in my whole life. That's why I'm imploring you to help me…just until I get through this…just till I get back on my feet again."

"When would you want to leave her with us?" Ross asked.

"I have her suitcase in the car," Melanie's eyes glistened, and she blinked as she fought against her tears.

Ross glanced at Maggie then returned his attention to Melanie. "We need to talk. Can you give us a little time alone?"

Melanie nodded. She started toward the porch steps.

Maggie had been silent, now she found her voice. "Thanks. We won't be long."

Melanie turned back to face them. She spoke softly. "I understand. I know I'm asking a lot, and I won't be angry with you if you feel you can't do this. I'm not sure how I'd react if I were in your place after our history. I'll wait in the car with Keri. You talk it over. But please, in view of everything else, know that I love my child dearly and want only the best I can provide for her. And right now, I feel that you, Maggie, and Ross are the best I can give her." There were tears rolling down Melanie's cheeks as she made her way down the porch steps. She walked toward her car and her sleeping child.

Ross reached for Maggie's hand, and they went into the living room. "This is anything but what I expected from her today. Not in my wildest imaginings could I have…" his voice trailed off.

Maggie shook her head. "I feel terrible for her and for Keri. She looks so ill. When she was explaining her condition to us I kept thinking, what if I had to face something like this? How frightening. It would be just awful, but I have you and wonderful support here in Serenity. She seems to feel she has no one."

"She's made some poor choices in her life, but I feel bad for her. She's from my past; you don't owe her anything. This is up to you, Maggie."

"I know." Maggie sighed. "But Ross, I think we have to help them. With her mother so sick, we have to try to provide some stability for Keri."

"Knowing you as I do, I thought you'd feel that way, Maggie. But it was only fair to you for us to talk in private. I love you so very much." He leaned closer and kissed her.

They discussed it for a few more minutes before they returned to the porch. Maggie beckoned to Melanie. Keri was awake and sitting in the front seat with her mother. They got out. Ross went to meet them. He caught Melanie's eye and nodded at her as they neared one another.

"Hi, Keri," he called out. "Do you remember me?" He asked as he reached the petite, blond, blue-eyed girl. It had been some time since they had last seen one another.

"I do," she said sounding very grown up. You're Ross, and you have the same last name as me. And you came to see me when I was in the hospital."

Ross knelt down and smiled at her. "You're right. Say...how would you like to go for a boat ride with me?"

A smile lit up her little face, and she turned to her mother. "Can I Mommy? Please?"

"I don't see why not. Put on a life jacket, and sit very still."

"I will. I promise." The child reached for Ross's hand, and they headed for the dock to the right of the property where a row boat was moored.

Melanie joined Maggie on the porch. She looked noticeably relieved. "I don't know how to thank you. I promise it won't be for long. And I'll call everyday."

Maggie reached out and embraced her husband's ex-wife. "You just concentrate on beating this, on getting rested and stronger. And I know it's a tall order, but try not to worry about Keri. We'll take good care of her for you."

Melanie took a tissue from her pocket and wiped her eyes. "I know, thank you," she whispered.

The two women looked out toward the small lake where Ross was rowing the boat toward the place where the stream widened. Keri's delighted laughter echoed back over the water. "I won't worry. I think she's going to be fine out here with you. And thanks again," she said giving in to tears, "I'll never be able to repay you."

...

A few minutes before the time Melanie planned to leave, she told Keri she had a big surprise for her. Keri was going to vacation, here at the lake with Ross and Maggie and their son Tyler. Keri was quite excited to meet their little boy. She frequently asked her mother for a brother or sister. Maggie told her they would go to get Tyler as soon as her mother left.

Melanie and Keri exchanged hugs and kisses and their customary, "I'll love you forever and ever and ever," ritual and she was fine with her mother's departure.

A short while later, the three of them drove into town to Caroline and Charlie's so Keri could meet Tyler. While Ross played a version of kickball with the children in the Keller's back yard, Maggie filled them in on the afternoon's events.

"Well, I'll be," Charlie said. "Who would have thought?" He shook his head.

"That's mighty nice of you and Ross, honey. I don't know if I could've been as charitable as you two after what she's done in the past." Caroline said. "You've taken on a lot of responsibility."

"Now, Caroline. You know you would have done the same for the child's sake, and for Melanie's." Maggie said. "Whatever else she's done, she's become a good mother, and she needs help. Look at that little girl out there, and think of how hard this is going to be for her. And think of what Melanie's facing."

Caroline softened. "You know I'll help you and Ross with this however I can." She was silent for a moment as she looked out the window before adding, "She's a pretty little thing, isn't she?"

"She is. And she's bright and very sweet." Maggie stepped closer to the backdoor and looked through the glass pane. "Look at them. They're having a great time together. Ross is so good with little ones."

Caroline and Charlie stepped to a kitchen window and looked out at the three of them running and laughing.

"That Ross, he's one in a million," Caroline said.

"Amen to that," Maggie's replied.

...

All was fine until bedtime that night. Tyler settled down after his evening ritual which Keri wanted to be a part of. She wanted Ross to hold her while Maggie rocked Tyler. As they were about to take her into her bedroom, the phone rang. It was Melanie. And she wanted to talk to Keri.

CHAPTER 13

As her mother tried to hang up, Keri began to cry. "No, mommy. Don't go! Come and get me." She wailed, and began to cry loudly. She pleaded repeatedly with Melanie to come for her and take her home.

Maggie and Ross could tell Melanie was trying to explain that she couldn't and say good-bye. Finally Keri dropped the phone to the floor. "She's gone," she sobbed. "Mommy's gone."

When Maggie tried to pick her up, she pushed her away and ran to Ross. "No! No! I want Ross!"

Maggie felt bad, but she certainly understood. She was a stranger to the little girl. Keri felt more comfortable with Ross from seeing him on several occasions. Now, he was her only security here away from her mother. It hadn't been bad during the day when they were playing and having fun, but bedtime could be a lonely time…a time when a child wanted her mother. She would have Ross ask Melanie to make her calls earlier in the day in the future. But for tonight, her mother was probably missing her terribly, too. And that was also understandable, especially with what she was facing. How lonely and frightening for Melanie too.

Ross sat with Keri on his lap. He promised her that they would go out in the boat again tomorrow. He rocked her until she fell asleep.

…

The next morning, Keri stood in the doorway and cried when Ross left for the pharmacy. Maggie left her alone for a few minutes as she cleared the table. Then she walked over and sat down on the floor a little distance from the child. Keri turned to look at Maggie but continued to wail.

Maggie began speaking in a soft, soothing voice. "You know what?"

"What?" Keri asked. Her sobbing subsided only enough to ask the question.

"I miss Ross when he goes to work, too."

The little girl looked at her. "You do?" She moved a tad closer to Maggie.

"Yes, I do. He's lots of fun to have around, isn't he?"

Keri stopped crying but continued to sniffle occasionally. "He plays good." She said in a tiny voice. She moved over beside Maggie.

"You know what I think we should do?" Maggie continued.

"What?" Keri wiped her eyes with the backs of her hands and dried them on her pajama legs.

"I think we should go upstairs and see if Tyler's awake. Then we can have breakfast. You get to pick whatever you want." After she said it, Maggie hoped she didn't ask for something she didn't have like cotton candy or a purple popsicle.

"Can I have French Toast?"

"Sure. I can fix that. Tyler loves it too."

"With sugar and lots of syrup?" Keri continued.

"If that's the way you like it…with sugar, and lots of Syrup." Maggie chuckled but grimaced inwardly as she thought of future dental bills. "After breakfast let's go into town. We'll go shopping, and we'll buy some things to fix your room just the way you want it while you're here."

A faint smile began to transform Keri's face. "Really? I can choose?"

"Yes. And then, we'll all go over to the pharmacy and see if Ross can have lunch with us."

She clasped her little hands together and a smile lit up her whole face as she got to her feet. "Yes! Let's go get Tyler now!"

As they started to Tyler's room, Maggie was touched to feel Keri's little hand slip into hers.

By the end of they day, Maggie and Keri had become fast friends and Keri referred to her as Aunt Maggie. Maggie was very relieved. And Tyler was overjoyed to have a new little companion who played with him constantly. Keri was quite the little mother, fussing over him, seeing to his needs even to the point of telling Maggie he needed a tissue when his nose ran.

...

On Tuesday, Lindsay called Maggie from the clinic on her lunch hour. "I would have called last night to let you know I was back but it was so late, I didn't want to disturb you."

"Did you have a good time?"

"Wonderful, and I want to tell you all about it but first, I hear you have some pretty big news of your own. What a difference a few days can make!"

"Word surely travels fast in this little town," Maggie said. "I assume you're referring to our new little house guest."

"I am. That just blew my mind when Kathryn told me."

Maggie filled her in on Melanie's visit and how things were going for them with the new living arrangements.

Then Lindsay said, "I hated to have to come home, and Tom said he hated to see me leave. He wants me to come back the next time he has a few days free. Oh, Maggie! He's so wonderful, and he makes me feel so special. And he's interested in everything about me and my life here in Serenity. Not like some men, totally absorbed in themselves."

"Does he have any idea when he'll be back this way to stay for a while?"

"No. He says at least another month. You know, I was just thinking. I'd like to take a drive over and see where he lives. I've never been there, but I have a good idea of where it is. I want to know everything about him. Would you and the kids be willing to ride over with me, maybe Saturday afternoon if Ross is working?"

"We'll see. Caroline had mentioned having the little ones over on Saturday for a couple of hours. If that works out, maybe the two of us can ride over to…what town did you say it is?"

"I'm not sure it's right in town. It's on the outskirts of Bromley from what he's said. I wouldn't think it would be too hard to locate. Unlike men, we can always ask directions if we need to."

...

Saturday dawned sunny but with a chill in the air, not unexpected for early November.

"I don't understand the point of driving over to see where he lives," Ross said as he and Maggie sipped their breakfast coffee.

"I guess it's a woman thing. She thinks she's falling in love with him and says she wants to know everything about him."

Ross shook his head and chuckled softly. "Okay. You two be careful. How long do you think you'll be gone? Will you be back when I get off today, or shall I stop for the kids?"

"No, we should be back in plenty of time for me to get them. I wouldn't think it would take more than a couple hours, no more than three at the most. It isn't too far from what she tells me, maybe twenty-five or thirty miles each way. Maybe we'll meet someone there who knows him and learn a little more about him from them."

"That's an idea. He's definitely something of a mystery man. Why don't you make a point of it?"

...

After leaving the children sitting at the kitchen table eating cookies and drinking milk with Caroline and Charlie, Maggie and Lindsay headed out of town.

"Thanks for driving, Maggie."

"No problem. This way you're free to take in everything about this trip. Now, tell me where I'm going."

Forty minutes later they drove into Bromley and stopped to eat lunch. Afterward they headed out of the city limits and turned down a country road. "He mentioned he turns onto the first road to the left after you leave town. Its a few miles down that road in a small development with only a few houses spaced out in it. I guess it's relatively new construction."

They drove on for five miles and didn't see housing area's that fit the description Lindsay was looking for.

Maggie finally said. "I'm going to pull off the next chance I get. We'll go back to that little gas station we passed and ask about it."

They continued on for another mile. "That's it. I'm turning around. We're way out of Bromley now."

Traffic was sparse so she had no problem turning on the road they were traveling. When they reached the combination convenience store/gas station, Lindsay went in. When she came out, she wore a frown.

She opened the car door and got in. "There's no where like that on this road. The clerk said we missed the first turn out of town, we took the second. He said lots of folks do. The first is a very narrow road and isn't well marked, sort of looks like a driveway with tall bushes around it."

Maggie glanced at her watch as she headed back toward Bromley. "I'm sure glad we stopped."

Lindsay noticed and said, "I know this has taken longer than you expected. We probably shouldn't have stopped to eat on the way. Let's just take a quick run by before we leave since we've come this far."

"Okay. I just don't want to leave the children too long. Caroline and Charlie are used to one, not two."

"I know, Maggie. I understand, and thanks."

They drove back toward Bromley. This time, they saw the turn. "I can understand how we missed it," Lindsay said. "If we hadn't stopped to ask, we'd never have found it."

Three miles down the road they came to a small development with five homes spaced on lots that appeared to be a couple of acres each. "There!" Lindsay said pointing to the most distant one. "That looks like it could be his from what he's mentioned about it. See the Oak tree and the side porch?"

There were no cars in the drive and no signs of life about the property.

"It's pretty," Lindsay said. "I think I could be happy there."

Maggie turned her head and smiled at her friend. "Can we go now?"

"Sure."

Maggie used the driveway next door to turn around. As they headed away from the development, a late model burgundy Mercury Marquee passed them on its way into the neighborhood.

Instantly, Lindsay turned in her seat to watch where it went. "Maggie! I swear that looks like Tom's car! And there's a man driving and a woman in the front seat with him!"

Maggie slowed her car to a crawl. The vehicle drove to the far house and turned into the driveway. It continued on toward the attached garage. They watched the garage door rise to admit the car and then close quickly restricting their view.

CHAPTER 14

"**Oh** my God, Maggie! Do you think that could have been him? Do you think that woman was his wife?"

Maggie pulled to the side of the road and stopped. When she looked at Lindsay, her friend's face was flushed. "Did it look like Tom to you?"

"I didn't get a good look at him. I only noticed the car as it reached us. I wasn't expecting to see it or him. Let's go back to the house."

"And do what?" Maggie asked.

"I don't know. Ring the bell…see who comes to the door."

"Lindsay, you don't really want to do this, do you? Wouldn't you rather think about it for a while? If it was Tom, and if that is his wife, there could be a logical explanation. I think we should go back to Serenity and give you some time to think before you do something you might regret."

Lindsay sighed deeply as she leaned back against the headrest. The two women sat in silence. Maggie waited.

Finally Lindsay said, "You're right. I have no idea what I'd say if he came to the door. And I don't have any claim on him. He's made no promises to me. And, he hasn't asked for any from me. Let's go home."

Maggie wanted to say something to comfort Lindsay but she couldn't think of anything. She decided to concentrate on her driving and let the conversation rest.

It was a much more silent ride home than it had been coming earlier in the day. When they reached her garage apartment, Lindsay said, "I'm going straight upstairs. I'll call you later."

Maggie noticed Lil's car parked near Caroline's back door as she went to pick the children up.

...

Later, at the house, the little ones napped while Maggie mixed up a meatloaf and her own special recipe for macaroni and cheese. Even if they didn't like the meatloaf, she figured all children love the pasta dish. At least that would be a hit.

The aroma of the combination was drifting through the house at 5:30 when Ross came in. "Hey, do I smell your meatloaf? It always makes my mouth water."

"A man after my heart…a man who loves my meatloaf!" Maggie laughed. "And macaroni and cheese to please Tyler and Keri."

"That'll please me too!" He said it as he bent down to kiss her. "So how was the excursion to check out the mystery-man's digs?"

"Not exactly what Lindsay expected. We had a heck of a time finding it and when we did…" The phone rang.

Ross lifted the receiver. "Hello. … Sure, she's right here. She was just about to fill me in on your adventure." He handed the phone to Maggie who was at his side by now.

"Hi. What's up?" She listened for a couple of minutes; then said, "Well good. See? Aren't you glad you didn't jump to conclusions and do something you'd regret?"

After they hung up, Maggie went to the cupboard and began removing dishes and glasses to set the table as she continued relaying her story of the trip to her husband. She concluded with what Lindsay had told her on the phone. She was so engrossed in what she was doing that she failed to notice Ross's frown as he listened to what Lindsay had told her.

CHAPTER 15

The plan for the next Sunday was to visit Melanie at her home a little north of Chapel Hill. She was feeling quite weak and was very lonely for Keri. The last time she and Maggie had spoken to make the plans, Melanie told her she had read something very hopeful in the newspaper and was praying that it would be of help to her.

"I'll tell you all about it when you get here."

The Harrington's planned to arrive around lunchtime and bring chicken in from the Colonel. As they turned onto Melanie's street, Keri became even more excited than she was when they told her about the visit earlier that morning.

"Mommy, Mommy! She said happily. "We're almost at Mommy's house…and mine," she said turning to Tyler and pointing. "See? That's my and Mommy's house right over there."

Tyler appeared not quite sure what all this excitement was about. Ross pulled into the driveway and turned the ignition off. Melanie appeared on the small front stoop of the modest brick home as Ross and Maggie got out of the car. While Ross took Tyler out of his car seat, Melanie helped Keri out of hers and covered her with kisses. Keri reach for her mother's hand and clung to her.

"Let's go in. I've been so excited waiting for you." Melanie and Keri led the way.

Dixie Land

Ross took the chicken and fixings out of the back and followed them up the stairs and through the door.

"Let me take that into the kitchen," Melanie said. "You all have a seat." Keri went into the kitchen with her mother.

When they returned, Maggie noticed how thin and tired Melanie still looked. She was wearing a wig today, a good match for her own color and style. When Melanie sat down in an easy chair, Keri climbed onto her lap. Maggie was so glad they'd agreed to come when she saw how happy they both were to be together again. It wasn't long until Tyler squirmed off his mother's lap and started exploring some of the small objects on the end tables.

"Please don't touch those, Tyler," Maggie said gently.

"Keri, why don't you take Tyler to your room?" Melanie said. "I bet he'd love to play with some of your toys?"

Keri kissed Melanie's cheek and reluctantly left her mother's lap. However, once down, she skipped off happily with Tyler right at her heels.

"They play great together, Mel," Ross said.

"They really do," Maggie agreed. "She's absolutely wonderful with him."

Melanie smiled. "I knew she'd be happy with you. She's been asking for a brother for the last year. I guess she thinks she's found one."

"Tell us how you're doing," Ross said. "I think you look a little more rested than the last time we saw you."

"I guess my body's adjusting a little. I think maybe I'm a bit stronger. I've been trying to work a couple of hours a day. The lab has been great. They've set me up with a network computer so I can operate from here when I feel like it. It's been wonderful, because I can work on my own schedule and not even dress if I don't feel like it."

"It's great that you have an employer who's willing to work with you like that," Maggie added.

"Tell us what you saw on the news that has you encouraged," Ross said.

"It was in the paper. And I'm excited because it's going on right here practically in my backyard."

"Now I do remember you did say you read it, in the *News & Observer,* I think you said?"

"There are some doctors at UNC here who have helped develop a genetic test that will help provide patients who have lung cancer and their physicians with information about lung tumors, including which type cells the tumors are and which types will respond to treatment. Lung cancer is such a deadly killer, there's only a five-year survival rate for 15% of its victims. Dr. David Neil Hayes is a Chapel Hill oncologist, and he's the lead investigator of the team that developed this. He's also the lead author of the paper that reported the results in an issue of the Journal of Clinical Oncology. I've read that too. He worked with colleagues at Harvard, John's Hopkins and several other schools of medicine. They used their testing to look at the genetic makeup of two-hundred-thirty tumor samples banked at various academic medical centers. They identified three distinct types of lung cancer tumors along with their genetic fingerprints.

"Anyway, to get to my point, a good friend of mine knows him personally, used to work for him, and she's going to introduce me to him. I'm hoping I can volunteer in some way to be part of their study." Melanie had brightened as she talked.

"Gosh, that sounds great, Mel. I hope it works out." Ross smiled at her. "I'm glad to see them working on this. It's such a deadly disease, it's one of the top killers in men and women."

"Lord what I'd give to have never seen a cigarette," Melanie said sadly. "When I was pregnant I quit, and didn't start up again but, for me, the damage had already been done, apparently. I pray every night that Keri won't ever start. I've already talked to her about it."

...

Dixie Land

It had been a pleasant afternoon. When it became apparent that Melanie was growing weaker, Ross said it was time for them to leave. She was becoming a little short of breath from all the excitement of the visit. They didn't want Keri to notice and become frightened. They promised to come back soon. There were tears when they parted but not as many as that first night Keri spent with them after Melanie brought her to them.

...

Maggie helped out at the church playschool on Monday. After she dropped Keri and Tyler off Wednesday morning, she did some shopping after which she stopped by Caroline and Charlie's to visit until time to pick them up. She filled them in on the visit with Melanie.

"It's still hard for me to think she isn't up to something," Charlie said.

"Believe me, she's ill," Maggie assured him. "If you saw her, you'd feel sorry for her. And she's trying to be brave and hopeful. I think having Keri, even though she thought she never wanted children when she was with Ross, has changed her. She's devoted to the child, that's apparent every time I see them together."

"Well, she is a sweet little girl," Charlie said. "I'll leave you two to your gossip. I'm going to work in the garden for a while." He grabbed a lightweight jacket and headed out the back door.

Caroline nodded. "Zip up," she called after him in a motherly tone. Then turning back to Maggie, she said, "Let me pour you a cup of coffee, Maggie. Sit down here at the table and fill me in on Saturday. You never really had much to say about Lindsay's and your trip to Bromley. And we haven't seen much of her this week to hear about it from her."

Maggie sat down and took a sip of the coffee Carolyn brought her. "At first, it appeared it was going to be a wild goose chase. We finally found the road where she thought his place was. We drove down and she thought she spotted a house that fit his description. As we were leaving we passed a car coming into the area. Lindsay thought it looked like Tom's. There was a man and a woman in it. It turned into the house she thought might be his. As you can imagine, she was pretty upset."

"I bet she was." Caroline shook her head.

"After I dropped her off at the apartment, she called Tom on his cell phone. She said she caught him at the airport; he was headed for Mexico on business. She seemed to feel better about the whole thing. She said she guessed it was just a coincidence seeing a man and woman and a similar car. And maybe that wasn't even his house. Anyway, all was well with her after they talked."

"I don't know, Maggie. The more time passes the more I distrust this guy," Caroline said. "I'm getting some bad vibes about this whole situation. Did you tell Ross about this? And, if you did, what did he think about it?"

CHAPTER 16

"I did. Ross didn't have anything to say. I think Lindsay's really infatuated with him and she'd like it to develop into something serious, but it hasn't yet. I think going slow is a good thing for both of them. She's been hurt and he's had a marriage that ended badly. And, as she admitted once we started back from Bromley, they haven't made any sort of a commitment to one another. I think the way she put it was, 'I don't have any claim on him. He's made no promises to me, and hasn't asked for any from me'."

"Well, just the same, she's very special to us and she had her heart broken once, I don't want that to happen again," Caroline said.

"I'll second that," Maggie said. "She's a terrific person, and she deserves someone just as special."

The phone rang and Caroline went to answer it. When she returned, she said, "That was Lil. She said Kevin called her and wants to come to Serenity later in the week. He wants her to invite all of us to Lil's for a party…at his expense. He has a special announcement to make, and he wants his aunt's dearest friends to be there when he makes it. He asked her to pick a day that's good for all of us and get back to Lil so she can let him know."

"I'll check our schedule with Ross and let you know what works for us, and I'd better check with Mildred to see when she can watch the children."

"Okay, honey. Any night's fine with Charlie and me."

Maggie glanced at her watch. "I need to go. Thanks for the coffee and conversation." They embraced, and Maggie stepped outside, waved at Charlie and got into her car.

...

That evening after the bedtime ritual had been completed and the children were asleep, Ross poured Maggie a glass of Cabernet and they went into the living room. Ross lit the gas logs and they sat together on the couch. After catching up on one another's day and deciding that Friday would work best for them to go to Lil's event, Ross brought up the topic of Lindsay.

"You know, the more I think about her relationship with this Tom character, the more I distrust him. He could have been anywhere when she called him on his cell phone. He could have told her he was at the airport, but he could have been next door to her or in Bromley for all she could prove."

Maggie shifted in her seat to look at him. "You too? Caroline is sort of concerned about that relationship also. Why didn't you say something the other day when I told you about our conversation?"

"Well it struck me as curious at the time. The more I thought about it, the more I wondered about him. As soon as he's about to meet her friends, he gets called away. She sees a car that looks like his on the street where she thinks he lives. There's a man and woman in the car. My gut instinct is check him out."

"How do we do that?"

"Well, Ryan and I switched days off so he could keep his dental appointment, so I'm free tomorrow. What do you say to us driving over to Bromley and asking a few questions?"

CHAPTER 17

It didn't work out for Ross and Maggie to make the trip the next day. Ryan had a problem at his dental appointment and had to travel to Fayetteville on Thursday to have a root canal. They decided to go the following Wednesday.

The week seemed to race by. Maggie and Lindsay didn't talk which was very unusual for them. Instead, they played telephone tag. Maggie was relieved in a way. She didn't want Lindsay to know what they were planning until they got back. If they found something of significance, she would tell her. If everything was okay, they would ease their own minds.

...

Wednesday morning, they dropped the children off at the church playschool. Caroline and Charlie would pick them up. Ross and Maggie reached Bromley at a little after ten.

"I'd say the place to start is City Hall," Ross said. "We'll look up the property records. You don't happen to know what his ex-wife's maiden name was, do you?"

"No. I don't know if Lindsay even knows. If she does, she hasn't mentioned it to me."

A thorough search of the records for the last six years turned up no property purchased by a Thomas Cullen, or any other Cullen for that matter.

"Let's go to the drug store down the street. I probably know the pharmacist, and I'll ask if anyone there knows of him.

This is a pretty small town, so I imagine most people know a lot of the folks who live here. That search turned up a blank also.

"Let's go to the library and get an old phone book and see if he's listed in it," Maggie suggested.

"Good idea." They inquired as to its location and reached it a few minutes later. Another dead end.

"Okay, let's check the city directory and see who lives at the address the two of you found the other day. Do you remember the street name?"

"Oh gosh, I saw it as we turned in. It was the name of some kind of tree, but I'm not sure which." Maggie stepped over to the librarian and described the location of the street.

"Oh, you mean Birch Lane," the woman at the desk said. That's a relatively new development. It was just annexed a couple of years ago."

They thanked her, found Birch Lane in the City Directory and copied down the five addresses and the names of the people who lived at them.

"Now let's go back to City Hall and see if any of these properties have changed hands recently," Ross said.

They left the library and headed back to check the records once again.

"You're mighty interested in the property here in Bromley," an elderly clerk said upon their return. "You two thinkin' about moving here?"

"Could be," Ross said. A bit of a mischievous grin turned the corners of his lips up.

Maggie nudged him. "Shame on you," she scolded under her breath.

That search turned up no mention of the name Tom or Thomas Cullen. Maggie removed a notepad from her purse and copied down the names of the property owners.

The two left, reached their car and headed out of town toward Birch Lane.

"What do we do when we get there?" Maggie asked. She glanced at her watch. "I doubt anyone will be here at this time of day. It was mid-afternoon when we saw that car the other day."

Ross turned onto Birch Lane and drove until they came to the five houses.

"There," Maggie said pointing to the last of the five homes, "that's it."

Ross drove to the house and pulled into the drive. He stopped in front of the garage doors. "You wait here," he said.

"What are you going to say if someone comes to the door and asks what you're doing here?" Maggie asked. She got no answer. The car door had already swung shut.

She watched while Ross rang the bell and then gave the knocker a couple of raps. No one answered. He walked down the front steps and peered in the garage window before returning to the car. There's one car in the garage, a Ford SUV.

"So now what?" Maggie asked.

"I don't know. We do know that there's no record of Tom owning any property anywhere in town in the last six years. We know the name of the family that lives here is Anderson. So, I don't guess we have much of anything."

Ross started the car, turned around in the wide area of the drive way and drove back to the street. He headed out of the subdivision slowly. There was an elderly woman standing at the roadside mailbox two houses down.

On impulse, Maggie said. "Ross, stop! I want to talk to that woman."

The car stopped. Maggie exited and walked across the street. "Hello." Maggie flashed her a bright smile. "I'm looking for someone who lived here recently. I hope you can help me."

The woman looked at her and took a few backward steps. Then she stopped in the driveway and returned Maggie's smile. "I might be able to, honey. I'm Ida. I live here with my son and daughter-in-law. Who is it you're tryin' to find?"

"It's a gentleman who used to own a house on this street. His name is Tom Cullen. He may have lived down there with his wife." Maggie pointed back toward the house at the end of the lane.

"Oh yes, I know who you're talking about. I'm here all day by myself so I keep a pretty good eye on this neighborhood. I know exactly who you mean. But he didn't own the house, and he didn't live there with no wife." The woman went on to give them quite an earful.

"I think I should tell Lindsay," Maggie said, as they drove back to Serenity. "He isn't being honest with her. If he's lying about this, who knows what other lies he's told her, and why?"

"How do you think she's going to react to it?" Ross asked. "Us having checked him out without telling her."

"I don't know. She's pretty crazy about him. But, because of that, I'd think she'd want to know before she gets in any deeper."

"When do you plan to talk to her? My suggestion would be to do it in person when you have a little time to spend with her."

"I agree. Maybe I'll go by tomorrow after she gets home from work or do you think I should wait until after the Friday shindig?"

"I don't know, Honey. You know her better than I do. It's your call."

...

Late Thursday afternoon Lindsay called Maggie. She was still at the clinic but was ready to leave. "There's something I need to talk to you about!" She sounded quite upset. She asked Maggie to meet her at her apartment as soon as she could get to town.

Has she somehow found out that Ross and I went to Bromley yesterday? Did that neighbor talk to the people who live in the house and tell them someone was enquiring about their "house guest? Is Lindsay angry

Dixie Land

with us? Is that why she sounded so upset and wanted to see me right away? Maggie's stomach churned as she drove into Serenity.

CHAPTER 18

Charlie was raking the grass along the side of the driveway when Maggie pulled up. "Hi there, little girl." A broad smile lit up his face. "You here to see us or Lindsay?"

Maggie stopped to chat for a moment. "Now Charlie, you know I'm always glad to see you. But Lindsay called earlier and asked if I'd come over. Said she needed to talk to me."

"Well, I'm glad she's talking to someone. She hardly gave me the time of day when she came flyin' in. Not like herself at all. Seemed pretty upset about something. Maybe she'll come down later and talk to Caroline."

"I'd better go on up now," Maggie said. "Tell Caroline I'll stop in before I leave."

Charlie returned to his raking, and Maggie went to the apartment door and rang the bell before starting up the enclosed staircase.

Lindsay was waiting for her as Maggie reached the landing. "Maggie. Come in."

"What's wrong?"

"I'm terribly upset, and I have a splitting headache."

Maggie followed her inside wondering what the next few minutes held for her.

"Have a seat, Maggie." Lindsay sat down in the nearest chair and Maggie went to the sofa.

"You sounded so upset on the phone." Maggie thought her friend looked as if she had either been crying or was on the verge of tears. "Tell me what's wrong."

"Something awful." She began to sob.

Maggie rose, went over and knelt beside her chair. She waited for Lindsay to continue.

"Oh, Maggie. I'm pretty sure I'm pregnant!" More sobs escaped her.

Maggie was stunned. This wasn't what she expected.

"And...and I've been trying to call Tom for the last two days, and he doesn't answer his phone. I've left messages but he hasn't returned my calls."

"What'd you say in the messages?"

"Just that I really need to talk to him, that it's very important."

"Perhaps he's somewhere that he isn't getting the calls."

"I hadn't thought of that. Maybe I should give him a while longer."

"Did he know how long he'd be out of the country?"

"He didn't say. Just said he'd be in touch when he could." She seemed to be calming a bit.

"Have you talked to Doc about this? Have you had him examine you?"

"No. Not yet. I know I should, but I just haven't been able to bring myself to talk to him about it yet. You're the only one I've told. I'm over three weeks late and I'm never late. I'm beginning to notice some little changes in my body, too."

Maggie stayed for another thirty minutes, listening to Lindsay, trying to comfort her. Of course, now wasn't the time to tell her about their excursion to Bromley and what they'd found. Lindsay didn't need any more stress on her now than she already had.

...

When Maggie reached home, Ross had fed the children. They were dressed for bed and ready for the evening ritual which Keri was now into as much as Tyler.

After the children were tucked in, they went downstairs. Ross gave Maggie the plate of food he had saved for her. He kept her company while she ate, and she filled him in on her conversation with Lindsay.

Ross shook his head. "I'm feeling worse about this the more it unfolds. And I feel bad for her. Is she sure she's pregnant?"

"Pretty sure. I told her to talk to Doc. That he was wonderful with me when I went to him when I first moved here. But, I think what has her most concerned is that suddenly she can't get in touch with Tom."

Ross was thoughtful for a moment. He shook his head without further comment.

...

Friday morning Maggie was dusting her living room tables when the door bell rang. She walked to answer it wondering who it could be. She hadn't heard a car approach the house or even a car door shut.

She peered through the privacy hole. It was their postman, Jake Witherspoon. She opened the door. "Hi Jake, what brings you to our door this bright sunny morning?"

"Registered letter for you." He held up an official looking envelope. "I need you to sign for it. Right here." He pointed as he made an 'X' and handed her the form to sign still holding onto the envelope.

Maggie complied and handed it back. He gave her the letter.

"See you," Jake said. He turned and left.

Maggie stepped inside and looked at the return address. "What in the world...? She said as she tore it open, unfolded the papers inside and began to read. "Oh no! No...no...no!" She made a dash for the phone.

Lil answered the pharmacy phone.

"Hi, Lil, it's Maggie. Is Ross handy?"

"He's on the other line, honey. Do you want to hold or shall I have him call you back? He's talking to a pharmaceutical company; don't know how long he'll be tied up."

"Have him call me as soon as he hangs up. It's really urgent."

"Are the children okay?"

"Yes, Lil. I just need to talk to Ross."

"Alright, honey. I'll have him call."

Maggie wanted to talk to Ross before she said anything to anyone else about this. She knew that soon it would become a matter of public knowledge but for now, they needed to think it through.

The phone rang ten minutes later. Maggie grabbed the receiver as the first ring ended. "Oh, Ross! It's terrible! Can you come home right away? We need to talk!"

CHAPTER 19

Ross laid the open letter down on the kitchen table. "Can he do it?" Maggie asked. "Does he have a right to?"

"I'd say the first thing we do is check the North Carolina law on child custody," Ross said. He rose from the table. "Let's go into the office and see what we can find about this on the internet."

Maggie followed at his heels as he entered his study and turned on his computer. She pulled a chair up beside her husband and they searched several areas of custody law.

"Ross, we can simply deny that he is Tyler's father."

"If you think that, you didn't read the whole letter, Maggie. He's requesting DNA testing and he knows he's the father and you know he is. We can't deny that."

"I have to admit, I didn't. The first few paragraphs made me so upset I just put it down and called you. It's been almost two years now. Won't the court want to know why he didn't come forward until now?"

"I really don't know. His attorney must have thought he had a shot at winning or he wouldn't have taken the case."

"Michael isn't fit to have Tyler…he's emotionally unstable," Maggie said angrily. "I say we go to court and expose his past."

"I agree with you. He isn't fit. But we did something we probably shouldn't have, something that he can use against us. I registered as Tyler's father on his birth certificate. And if he pushes it and demands DNA testing, that could be a problem for us. But it probably wouldn't be since we were married at the time."

"In addition, Michael was unstable at the time...in rehab for a number of things, and in trouble with the IRS."

"But the fact remains that he is still Tyler's biological father."

"What are we going to do, Ross?"

Ross stepped over to her and wrapped his arms around her pulling her close to him. Maggie sobbed softly against her husband's shoulder. "This is just the worst thing I could have imagined," she whispered.

...

Ross finished dressing for Lil's party before Maggie did and went downstairs to wait for the babysitter to arrive. The doorbell rang as Maggie joined him in the living room. Mildred was going to watch the children tonight and she bustled in with treat bags for each of the little ones.

"Well, where are they?" She asked grinning. "I was sure they'd meet me at the door."

Maggie smiled at her. "They're in the playroom over there."

As she spoke, Tyler and Keri hurried into the living room. "Aunt Millie," they cried in unison.

Ten minutes later, Ross and Maggie were in their car heading down the highway to Lil's. Maggie broke the silence. "I'm planning to do something tonight I never thought I'd even consider again. I hope I'm making a wise decision."

Ross and Maggie were the last to arrive at Lil's. Lil opened the door to greet them as they reached the top step. "I was about to call you and see if you were still coming," she said as she gave Maggie a hug.

"We had a slight hold-up, but we certainly wouldn't have missed it. I guess I should have called." Maggie tried to sound carefree, she felt anything but.

Maggie saw Kevin across the room. Their eyes met, and he started toward them.

"Maggie, Ross. I'm so glad you came. He extended his hands to them, then turned and beckoned to a woman of perhaps twenty-eight or thirty who had just stepped into the living room from Lil's kitchen.

She joined them. Kevin said, "Carlie, this is the couple I've told you about, Ross and Maggie Harrington. Carlie is very special to me," Kevin said. He reached for her hand.

"Hi. I'm so glad to finally meet you two," Carlie said. "Kevin has told me a great deal about you. How good you are to his aunt, and what a rocky beginning he had with you. We're both glad you came tonight." Her green eyes seemed to twinkle, or was it just the lighting in Lil's living room? She wasn't really what most would call beautiful, but she had a warmth and kindness about her that was engaging. When she smiled, her entire face lit up and Maggie felt compelled to return the pleasantry.

"We really did have a bad beginning. And it was entirely my fault," Kevin said. "It's one of the reasons I wanted Lil to invite everyone here tonight."

Doc, Kathryn and the Townlees joined the little group. Kevin said, "Everyone please go into the dining room and get some refreshments. When you come back, I have something to say to all of you."

"Yes, do," Lil added. "I've fixed a plenty, so I hope you all came hungry."

Once everyone was comfortably seated, Kevin cleared his throat. He stood in the large, arched opening between the dining and living room so he had a clear view of all the guests. The room fell silent.

"I think what I'm about to say is long overdue. I wanted you all here tonight so I could apologize to you. I feel I let you all down a couple years ago. I came back to Serenity to reestablish my relationship with Aunt Lil for the wrong reasons. I'm sorry for it."

"Kev," Lil began.

He held up his hand. "Aunt Lil, please let me finish. I wanted to see my aunt, but I also came to learn more about Maggie for a client. I let a lot of people down, and I'm sorry. I had some pretty rough years when I was a teen, no dad, losing my mom. But my aunt and uncle took me in and gave me a home. And, though she wasn't my blood aunt, she was my supporter and my rock. I ran away from that when things got tough with Uncle Henry. I just added to her problems, Aunt Lil didn't deserve that. I lucked out in finding a friend whose family took me in, raised me as their own and saw to it that I got a good education. My priorities were misguided for quite a while. Then I met a wonderful lady…" he paused and reached out to Carlie. She stepped to his side. Kevin slipped his arm around her shoulders. "A wonderful lady who helped me realize the true value of love and trust. She helped me realize how truly blessed my life had been. Because of her, I decided I would do whatever it took to make amends for the years of worry I caused my aunt and to ask her forgiveness here with her dearest friends present. And I'm asking for all of you to forgive me too, especially Maggie… and Ross."

No one stirred, and no one uttered a sound.

"I guess that's about it," Kevin said softly.

"You know I forgive you, Kev. And I know how hard it was for you to come here tonight and…" Lil's voice trailed off as Maggie stood solemn-faced, and looked directly into Kevin's eyes.

CHAPTER 20

Kevin met her gaze. He said nothing as he waited for Maggie to begin.

Ross stood and took Maggie's hand.

"Kevin," Maggie said. "I...I trusted you once, and it hurt me. But, I believe you really are a different person now. You've earned Lil's trust and she's so happy to have you in her life again. I'm willing to leave the past behind us and start again. I think Ross will agree with me." As she finished speaking, she looked up into Ross's eyes.

He kissed her forehead. "Yes." He nodded. "Maggie speaks for both of us."

Kevin stepped forward and embraced Maggie lightly. "Thank you," he said softly. Ross reached out and the men shook hands.

It was an emotional moment in the room until Lil stepped toward the dining room and, sounding very motherly, said. "Finish up what you have on your plates and come back for more. I don't want this food to go to waste."

Maggie noticed Lil turn to her side slightly and wipe her eyes. Maggie knew it hadn't been easy for Kevin to apologize so publicly. This was the first time they'd seen him since all the turmoil that had surrounded their previous relationship. He couldn't have been sure how Maggie and Ross would react to him. He had been courageous to invite them tonight. She gave him credit for his effort. He seemed very sincere. She hoped for all their sakes that he was.

The evening was enjoyable, and the time passed quickly. At 11:00, Maggie and Ross said they needed to call it a night. Everyone else seemed to have been waiting for someone to start the exodus, as they all followed suit. Suddenly the Harrington's found themselves the last of the guests at the door with Lil, Kevin and Carlie. As the group stepped onto the front porch, Maggie asked Kevin if she could speak to him briefly.

"Certainly." They stepped back into the living room.

"Kevin, I have to ask you. When was the last time you had any contact with Michael?"

Without any hesitation he answered. "It's been a long time, Maggie. After your wedding, I represented him and got his situation worked out with the government. You know what happened there. He got a payment plan worked out and he agreed to go into treatment for his addictions. After I accomplished that for him, I severed our relationship. We weren't good for one another, and I didn't want any more involvement with him. He has respected that. Why do you ask?"

"Because. Today I received a letter from Michael's attorney. He's asking for rights with Tyler. He wants joint custody of him as his birth father. The thought of it makes me physically ill. I don't think he's changed. Tyler knows only one father. And that's Ross. They absolutely adore one another."

Kevin let out a low whistle. "I wouldn't have expected that of Michael. He never seemed one to want much responsibility when it came to kids or being faithful to one woman."

"You're right about that." Maggie looked away from Kevin as Ross stepped to her side.

"Did I miss something here? I thought we were leaving."

"I was just telling Kevin about our problem with Michael."

"Any advice to offer? We don't have a lot of time, only thirty days." Ross said.

"That's not my field. But I do have a friend whose specialty is family law. He's excellent, really knows all the ins and outs. I'll be glad to give you his contact information. In fact, I'll talk to Ben about your situation and get back to you after I do. Sort of set the scene and then you can get in touch with him."

...

As soon as they got into the car Ross said, "I'm surprised you told Kevin about our letter from Michael."

She sighed. "I thought about it before I did. And then I decided what could it possibly hurt? It isn't like the situation before when there was something Michael didn't know. This is out in the open. Michael knows the facts, and I thought possibly Kevin could be of help. I can't imagine how it could hurt us."

...

Ross and Maggie planned to take the children to visit Melanie on Sunday. She called them Saturday afternoon to tell them she was much weaker. She had seen her doctor again and the news wasn't good.

When they arrived at her home and rang the bell, Melanie called out, "Come in. The door's unlocked."

They stepped into the living room to find Melanie lying on the sofa. She was dressed in a pink silk robe and had a pink fleece blanket pulled up around her waist. It was obvious to Maggie that she was wearing a wig. She looked ashen even with make-up.

Her smile was genuine as she reached her frail arms out to Keri. The child ran to her mother and hugged her neck, then lay against her for a moment.

When she looked up into her mother's face she frowned. "What's wrong, Mommy? Are you sick today?"

Melanie blinked to hold back the tears that formed in her eyes. "Mommy doesn't feel very good today, but I feel lots better seeing you."

Tyler wanted a hug too, and that seemed to please Melanie. "What a big boy you're becoming. And so strong!" She said as he released his grip on her neck.

A short while later the children were off to Keri's room to play with her toys. Melanie pulled herself to a sitting position on the couch. "Things are looking very dismal for me. That study I told you about, the one for identifying the various kinds of lung cancer cells and their response to different treatments…well, it's too much in its infancy to be of any help to me. My doctor was very frank with me when I saw him on Friday. We discussed my alternatives. He mentioned Hospice and after reflecting on it, I've decided that's what I'm going to do. No sense continuing the chemo when it clearly isn't helping. And I'm tired of feeling miserable constantly. I want to be as comfortable as I can for whatever time I have left." Melanie was unable to hold back her tears any longer.

Maggie stepped over to the couch and sat down next to her. "I'm so sorry, Melanie. I wish there was something we could do or say that would help you in some way."

"There is. Ross…Maggie, I want you to adopt Keri. I want it to be all legal and binding before I die. Please!"

Maggie and Ross looked at one another. Maggie had tears in her eyes. Ross remained silent having already made his decision, but he felt it all depended on Maggie's desires.

"We've come to love Keri," Maggie said. "I love her. Tyler already thinks of her as his big sister. We'd love for her to be our daughter."

Ross went to Maggie's side and kissed her forehead.

Melanie appeared much relieved as she wiped the tears from her cheeks. "I prayed you would. I'm so grateful to you both. I wish things had been different. I wish…" Her voice trailed off.

The children rejoined them soon after, and Melanie seemed a little energized after their talk. When the time came to leave, Keri went to Melanie and wrapped her arms around her mother's neck. "I want to stay with you, Mommy, please."

"Keri, darling. Mommy is still feeling very sick. I want you to stay too, but I can't take care of you right now. And besides," she smiled at her child. "What would Tyler ever do without you?"

Keri looked at the little boy. "He does need me to take care of him and play with him."

Tyler looked at her and grinned. Then he ran over to her and gave her a bear hug.

When Melanie and Keri said good-bye, she held her daughter ever so tightly and whispered "I love you. I'll love you forever and ever and ever." Keri whispered it back to her. It was something they had said to one another since Keri learned to talk. Today it had an extra special meaning for Melanie.

Before they left, Melanie told them she would contact a lawyer first thing Monday morning and get the paperwork started.

As they drove to Serenity, the children watched the DVD of *Happy Feet*. It was their current favorite, and they had watched it so often they could almost repeat the dialogue word for word. It gave Ross and Maggie a chance to talk privately.

"I can't tell you how much it means to me for you to want Keri," Ross said.

"Of course I want her. It breaks my heart that she's going to lose her mother."

Ross reached for her hand and brought it to his lips. "For some reason you and I can't seem to make a little one of our own right now, but our family's growing just the same."

Maggie smiled. "We'll do that too, in due time."

They stopped to eat supper on the way home so that when they reached the house they could get the little ones off to bed. When they went back downstairs Ross poured them each a glass of wine. He started a fire in the fireplace and sat down on the sofa. He patted the seat next to him. "Come over here and enjoy the fire with me, Mrs. Harrington."

Maggie started to join him then noticed the blinking light on the telephone. "Let me check this message, and I'll be right there." She put the phone on speaker and dialed in the code. They heard a man's voice say, "Hi, Maggie and Ross. It's Kevin. I have some disappointing news for you. Please return my call at your earliest convenience." He left them a home, office and cell phone number.

CHAPTER 21

"What now? Do you want to call or shall I?" Ross asked.

Maggie sighed. "I will." She put the phone on speaker so Ross could hear the conversation. She dialed Kevin's home number. He answered on the third ring.

"We just got home from visiting Melanie. What's your news?"

"Aunt Lil told me a little about her problem and also that you are keeping her child until she's better."

"It looks like we'll be keeping her permanently. Melanie is going into Hospice care."

"I'm truly sorry to hear that. She seems to have straightened out her act and now this. But I don't want to keep you in suspense. What I called to tell you is that Ben is representing Michael."

"But Michael's lawyer's name is Robert, I'm sure." She turned back toward Ross who had already started for the desk to retrieve the envelope from the middle drawer. He removed the letter and handed it to his wife.

She checked the signature. "It says here B. Robert Barnes."

"I'm sorry, Maggie. I've always known him as Ben. He goes by Robert in his law practice. There was another Ben with the firm when he joined them so he opted for his middle name.

I'm working on finding someone else for you who is well qualified."

"Money isn't an issue for us, Kevin. We want the best attorney you can possibly find to represent us. We'll do some checking, too."

"Back to Melanie, you say you'll be keeping her child?"

"Yes. Melanie's asked us to adopt Keri. And we've agreed. It's a terribly sad situation."

"I agree. Life isn't fair. There was a bit of sadness in Kevin's voice, and then he returned to business. "I'll be back in touch with you in the next couple of days, Maggie."

"Thanks," the Harrington's said in unison. Kevin said goodbye and Maggie broke the connection.

She went over and sat down beside Ross. She reached for her wine goblet and took a sip. "I guess we shouldn't be surprised. Knowing Michael, he would seek out the best representation available and, since he was the instigator, he had plenty of time to research the field."

"Don't worry, honey. We'll find someone just as good, and we're going to win. Michael's past is much too shady to get very far with this. The truth will come out."

"I hope you're right, Ross." Maggie sighed. "I wonder where his money for this lawyer is coming from. Do you suppose he's back practicing medicine somewhere?"

"Hard telling when it comes to Michael."

"I wonder how much of a problem this adoption is going to be. Do you think Melanie can just phone a lawyer and make her wishes known, and it'll be a relatively simple thing?"

Ross thought for a moment. "Well, under the circumstances, I don't think it should be too complicated. Melanie is dying. She wants her only child to have the man and woman of her choice raise her daughter. We're in agreement. Keri is happy here with us. I don't see how there could be much of a problem. But then who know how the law works in cases like this. I'm sure she'll make a provision in the paperwork for the possibility of her recovery. It could happen, though it seems very unlikely with the kind of cancer she has."

"And if she does, of course, we would release her from the agreement," Maggie added.

"We would, but it should all be spelled out in black and white just the same," Ross continued.

"The only hang-up could be Keri's birth father," Maggie said. "We know who he is, but can we be absolutely sure he doesn't know?"

"I wonder who she named on the birth certificate," Ross said. She didn't know at the time Keri was born." He was thoughtful for a moment before adding, "she could have just made up a name."

"When she calls us again, I'll ask her," Maggie said. "I'll tell her that's the only problem we worry about with this adoption."

...

Melanie called late Monday afternoon. "I've talked with a lawyer by telephone. I explained the situation to him. After we spoke for a few minutes, he put his secretary on the line. She asked me a number of questions which I answered. She asked if I could come by the office. I told her I didn't know from day to day what I'd be capable of. She told me that for a charge, she could come to me and finish the paperwork and then take it back to the attorney to complete. She said when he completed it she'd bring the forms for us to sign. She also said that drawing up the paperwork doesn't take long but that waiting for the papers to be signed in court can drag on for a long time especially in a case where the birth father isn't in on it. But she said once the papers are drawn up initially she'd bring them at a time when you and Ross could be here also."

"That sounds fine, Melanie. It might be a good idea to put it in your will also. At any rate, let us know when the papers are ready, and we'll be there. And, speaking of the birth father,

Ross and I thought of that being a possible problem after we left you yesterday."

"How?" Melanie asked.

"Who did you name as Keri's father on her birth certificate?"

"It was embarrassing for me, but I listed him as unknown."

"Well, I'm sure you aren't the only woman who's done that." Maggie's tone was sympathetic. "I've been thinking of something else since Sunday. How are we going to handle telling Keri about this? How are we going to prepare her?"

CHAPTER 22

"That's something I've tried not to think of. But, I know I have to face it and before long. Give me a little more time with it. Perhaps you, Ross and I can share ideas about it when you come to sign the adoption papers. I think it might be best if the little ones don't come on that trip."

"I agree." Maggie added, "Oh, there's one more thing. Did you make a provision for the possibility that you may recover?"

"Yes. The attorney suggested that also. He said he'd put in a clause to cover it."

...

Tuesday morning Lindsay phoned. Maggie was on her way out the door to take Tyler and Keri to playschool. "Maggie, I need to talk to you."

"I'm running late," she told Lindsay. "What if I stop by the clinic after I drop the children off? Maybe you can take an early lunch and we can talk then."

"Sounds great. We aren't too busy today. I think Kathryn will cover for me for a half hour or so."

"I'll stop by for you, see you in a while," Maggie said.

Maggie had to wait for fifteen minutes before Lindsay was free to leave. They drove down to the *As You Like It* café.

After they found a table and gave their order, Maggie asked, "What's up?"

"I finally heard from Tom. He's back from his last business trip. I told him I needed to talk to him, and he said he had something important to talk to me about too. Oh, Maggie. I think I'm going to like what he has to say. I could tell by his tone, he was so warm. He said he had missed talking to me."

"That's great, Lindsay. Perhaps we can all get together while he's in town."

"I hope so. He'll be here through the weekend. We're going to meet at The Evergreens on Friday." Lindsay said. Her smile was bright, her cheeks flushed and her eyes sparkled.

Maggie was tempted to ask her why Tom always wanted to meet her somewhere, but she resisted the urge. She also decided not to tell her about her problems with Michael right now. Let Lindsay enjoy her own moment. She had a big problem, and it looked as if it would be solved when she and Tom got together again. At least Maggie hoped it would.

They had a very pleasant lunch. Afterward, Maggie dropped her friend off at the clinic, and then she headed for Caroline's. She had thirty minutes before she had to pick Tyler and Keri up. Just enough time to bring the Kellers up to date.

While she and Caroline were visiting, Ross called her on her cell phone.

"I've found an attorney. He's from a small town west of us but he has an excellent record. His name is John Barrow. I didn't want to wait for Kevin to come up with someone. I called him and told him I'd engaged John. Kevin said he only knows him by reputation, and that's why he didn't think of him right off. He said the guy knows his family law backward and forward."

"That's great, Ross. It makes me feel a little better."

"We have an appointment with him a week from Thursday in the afternoon."

"That's too far off. We only have thirty days to respond."

"I told him that. He said we can get another thirty days if we apply for an extension. Said it's an easy matter. He also said if he has a cancellation, he'll have his paralegal call us and schedule us in. Her name is Shelly."

"I'll see if Caroline and Charlie can watch the children for us." She and Ross said goodbye.

"You know I'll watch the little ones for you! Just tell me when."

Maggie gave her the details then turned to the topic of Lindsay and Tom. "I don't know what to make of him. Again, she's meeting him somewhere. Has he ever come here to pick her up for a date?"

"Not when we've been home, he hasn't. She always meets him out of town, somewhere between here and Bromley. She says it's because there's really nowhere to go in Serenity, and it saves time if they meet closer to where they're going to spend the evening. I guess they meet in the middle to make it closer for both of them. I must admit, I have a real curiosity about that fellow."

"Well, no matter where they're going, it seems strange to me that he never comes here. My mom always used to tell my sister and me, 'If a young man can't come to our door for you, you don't go out with him.'"

"I think it's a different world today, Maggie. You know, she's never been to his place either." Caroline added. "Just visited him in a hotel in D.C. I can't help but wonder if he's hiding something."

...

The Evergreens
Friday Evening

Tom's vehicle was parked in the Evergreen's lot when Lindsay pulled in and found an empty space. When she emerged from her car and started for the restaurant door, Tom opened his door and called to her. "Over here!"

"Tom!" She said turning around. "I'm late. I thought you'd already be inside."

Dixie Land

He got out and walked toward her. They met near his car. He reached out to her, pulled her to him and kissed her. "I've missed you, Lindsay Payne," he said, holding her close.

"I've missed you, too." Her lips met his again.

"Let's sit in the car for a minute. I want to talk to you." As he opened the door on the passenger side, she noticed he was driving the burgundy Mercury Marquee. Though she found it most curious, she didn't say anything. She waited for him to go around and get in his side.

"I'm so glad you're back. How long can you stay?" she asked.

"I think for a while, but of course that could change with a phone call. I have some decisions to make, and that's what I want to talk to you about." His expression and tone had become very serious.

Lindsay waited for him to continue. Her heart rate accelerated as she waited for the words she was longing to hear from him. She wanted him to propose to her without knowing she was pregnant. She didn't want him to feel forced into marrying her.

He turned in his seat to face her and reached for her hand. His dark eyes were highlighted by the brilliant restaurant marquee near by.

She smiled into his handsome face. "Yes."

"Lindsay, these last months of having you in my life have been wonderful. You're so vivacious, so spontaneous, such wonderful company. You've come to mean a great deal to me and…" he paused and looked down.

"I feel the same," Lindsay whispered.

"Wait, please let me finish. What I was about to say is, that's what makes this so hard for me to say."

CHAPTER 23

When Lindsay reached Serenity, she drove on through and straight to Maggie and Ross's. She parked her car, dashed up the front steps and rang the bell. She waited impatiently for someone to answer the door. Momentarily it opened and Ross, seeing it was Lindsay, stepped aside, "Hello! Come on in." His smile faced when he looked into her eyes.

Maggie reached the entryway behind her husband. "Lindsay, you've been crying. What on earth happened tonight?" She stepped forward and embraced her friend.

"Oh Maggie, It was awful! It didn't go at all the way I expected the evening to go." She began to sob.

Ross said, "I'll go into my office and leave you two gals alone. You know where I am if you need me."

"Thanks, Ross," Lindsay managed weakly before she sank down onto the couch and dissolved into tears.

Maggie sat down beside her. She waited for Lindsay to gain enough control of herself to tell her about the evening.

After a short while, Lindsay began to speak softly. "Tom was so romantic when I first saw him, said he'd missed me. Said all kinds of nice things to me. He made me feel so happy, built up my expectations." Lindsay sniffled and took a Kleenex from box on the coffee table and dabbed her cheeks and beneath her eyes. "But he was only saying those things to soften the blow of what he had to…to… tell me." She had started to sob again, and her words became inaudible.

Maggie reached for her forearm, stroked it gently and said, "I'm so sorry. I'm so sorry that he hurt you."

Lindsay began again. "He told me his ex-wife has been calling him…that she thinks she made a big mistake by letting him go and that…that she wants them to try again. Oh, Maggie, that hurt so deeply."

"And, is he going to give her another chance?"

"He is." She half spoke, half sobbed. "He said they had so many years of their lives invested in one another that they both felt they owed it to themselves to give it another try." She broke down again. "I'm sorry," she murmured. "But that's just the last thing I expected to hear from him tonight. From what he said, I thought they were over and done with for good…or I'd never have gotten involved with him."

"Then you didn't tell him you're pregnant?"

"No. How could I after that? I don't want someone who doesn't want me. I don't want him to feel trapped into marrying me…to feel sorry for me. No, I'll keep that to myself. I'm going to move back to Chapel Hill and get a job at the hospital there. I know they'll hire me back. They said they would when I left. I'll raise my baby there, and we'll be just fine. We won't be that far from you. After the baby's a little older, we'll come back and visit and I'll just tell people that the father and I came to a mutual agreement to dissolve our relationship."

"Lindsay, I wish you'd stay here. Ross and I could help you, and you know Caroline and Charlie would love to have you stay on there. They'll love your baby just as they do ours."

"I don't think so. But I'm not making any firm decisions right now. I'm too upset. I'll consider it. And I'll probably talk to Caroline tomorrow, but I wanted to talk to you first."

"Please stay the night with us in one of the guest rooms? You're much too upset to drive home. And you don't need to be alone tonight."

"Thanks, but no. I'll be alright. Maybe I'll talk to Caroline tonight."

Maggie glanced at her watch. "I'm sure they'll still be up. It's only 9:00. They rarely go to bed before the 11:00 o'clock news is over."

Lindsay rose; Maggie stood and followed her to the door. "He was driving that burgundy Marquee. I'm wondering if it might have been his wife's car all along."

Her words struck a distant cord with Maggie. The picture of the burgundy Mercury passing them with the man and woman in it flashed in her mind's eye. Then, she recalled the earful she and Ross got from the neighbor the day they visited Bromley.

Maggie walked to the door with Lindsay when she left. "Call me when you get to town so I know you're okay."

"I will."

Maggie closed the door and went to Ross's office. She was eager to get Ross's take on everything Lindsay had told her tonight including about the car Tom was driving when he met her at The Evergreens!

CHAPTER 24

Over the next couple of days Maggie and Ross heard nothing from John Barrow or his assistant about any cancellations. Maggie decided to call his office to check for herself. No one had cancelled. It appeared they would have to wait until the following Thursday. Maggie was disappointed. She hadn't heard anything from Melanie on the adoption process either.

When Ross's Wednesday afternoon off rolled around, he and Maggie decided to make a trip back to Bromley. They would go to the woman's home they had spoken with on the last trip and see what more they could learn from her. Once they gathered all their information and checked it out, Maggie had decided she would go to Lindsay with what she had learned.

As agreed, Caroline and Charlie would pick the children up from playschool and watch them until their parents returned. They knew Maggie and Ross's destination but vowed to keep their secret. Even one slip of the tongue in Serenity could result in half the town knowing what was going on. And both were relieved to know the situation was being checked out by someone who cared about Lindsay. They felt if anyone could get to the bottom of the mystery of Tom Cullen, Maggie could. People seemed to find it easy to confide in her.

...

There was very little traffic on the road Wednesday afternoon and Ross and Maggie reached Bromley in good time.

They drove through town and headed straight for Birch Lane. They drove to the second house from the end on the right. Ross pulled into the driveway and Maggie got out, ascended the front steps and rang the doorbell. She waited then rang the bell several more times before turning to leave. She was half-way down the steps when the front door opened partially, then wider and an elderly lady said, "Can I help you, Miss?"

Maggie turned back to see the woman she had met at the mailbox previously. She was wearing a flowered housecoat and blue slippers.

"Yes. Hello. Do you remember me? I'm Margaret. We spoke a few weeks ago at your mailbox. I was hoping you could answer a few more questions for me about your neighbors."

The woman appeared quite serious as she peered at Maggie. She reached into her pocket, removed a pair of glasses and put them on. Then her face relaxed into a smile. "Sure, I remember you, honey. You were looking for the man who's a house guest next door sometimes."

"Yes. That's right. He's a good friend of a friend of ours. She wanted us to contact him. We thought maybe the neighbors could help us. I wondered if you could tell me the name of your neighbors and where they work. It's really quite important." Maggie didn't like to be untruthful, but she was convinced it was a necessity in this case.

"I thought I told you their names before… but maybe not. Daniel and Evelyn Anderson. They own and operate a small private nursing home about six miles from here. He's the administrator and she's the personnel director. It has a good reputation, too." She shook her head. "Hasn't been open all that many years, but it's beautiful and it's expensive, I hear. Mighty expensive!"

"If you told me, I forgot. Did you tell me the name of the nursing home?"

"They call it Birchwood something. I heard they named it after this street. They were the first ones to build here and they named our street too."

Maggie felt exhilarated. "I can't thank you enough. Thanks so much for your help. I won't keep you any longer. I'm afraid I woke you from a nap."

"No problem, honey. It was time to get up anyway." She glanced at her watch. "Almost time for my soap opera, so you did me a favor."

"Thanks again." Maggie turned and started down the steps.

The woman pushed the door partway shut then stuck her head through the opening and called out, "By the way, that young man was just here visiting last weekend. I almost forgot to tell you that."

Maggie stopped. "Do you think he might still be here?"

"I don't think so. I saw him go out carrying two suitcases Monday afternoon. Seemed to be in a real hurry.

...

Fifteen minutes later, Maggie and Ross pulled into the large parking area of Birchwood Manor. The facility was an expansive, two story, pristine-white building with twelve immense white circular columns stretched across the front. It immediately put Maggie in mind of Tara in *Gone with the Wind*. Only, it was much larger. The grounds were lovely with plantings throughout the islands that divided the rows of spaces in the parking lot. There was more colorful foliage tastefully positioned under each window around the building. The second story rooms had French doors that lead to balconies off of each room. Maggie guessed it could house sixty to eighty residents depending on how many double rooms it had.

"When their neighbor said expensive, she hit it on the head. This is lovely but I'm sure it costs a pretty penny to live here," Maggie said.

Ross parked the car. "Do you want to go in or shall I? Or, we could go together."

"Let me go alone," Maggie said. "I think one on one might be better."

...

Maggie stepped into a beautiful living room with plush, burgundy colored carpeting, comfortable looking cream colored leather furniture and an ornate chandelier hanging from the twelve foot ceiling.

Maggie was still taking it all in when she heard the woman at the information desk just inside the room say, "Welcome to Birchwood. May I help you?"

"Yes. I'm Margaret Harrington. I'd like to speak with Mr. Anderson for a few minutes if he's available."

She smiled at Maggie and asked, "Do you have an appointment?"

"No. I just took a chance that he'd be able to see me."

"Is this in reference to a position here? Are you answering our ad?"

"I'm not answering the ad."

"Do you wish to obtain information for a family member?"

"No. I…"

"Are you from the state?" The woman asked. Her manner had cooled considerably with her last question.

"No, none of those. May I please speak with him? It's personal. It won't take long."

The woman eyed Maggie warily for a moment. "You can have a seat over there," she said gesturing across the room to a chair. Maggie complied and the woman lifted the receiver from her desk phone, punched in an extension and turned her head away from Maggie. She spoke very softly into the receiver.

Strange, Maggie thought. A few minutes later, a tall, slender, stunning blond appeared through one of the doors to the side of the living room. She walked over to Maggie. She reached out her hand as Maggie stood.

"I'm Evelyn Anderson," she said. Maggie took her hand. "Mr. Anderson is tied up this afternoon, but I'll be glad to help you if I can."

...

When Maggie rejoined Ross, she felt relieved to be out of Birchwood Manor.

"I had an eerie feeling the whole time I was in there. The secretary acted as if she didn't trust me…as if they were suspicious of me."

"Really? Were you able to find out anything about Tom Cullen?"

"Not much. I didn't get to see the administrator. His wife came out and told me he was tied up. I told her I was trying to contact a mutual friend of ours. I gave them his name and she said she personally didn't know him well. That he was a friend of her husband and she didn't know how to contact him. That he only visited occasionally and that's all she would say."

"We knew that much when we came," Ross said.

"I don't buy for a minute that she doesn't know him very well if, as the neighbor said, he's been a frequent house guest."

"I agree. She obviously wasn't about to give you any information."

"Right. She said she was sorry she couldn't be of more help and promptly began walking me to the door. I felt kind of foolish. But I also got the feeling that she was uncomfortable with my visit. When I thanked her and reached out to shake her hand as I was leaving, her hand had turned quite cold."

"Hmmm. It does seem strange," Ross said. "But it doesn't appear there's anything we can do about it for now."

...

Several days following their visit Maggie opened the morning newspaper, and it all became perfectly clear why the people at Birchwood Manor behaved as they did last week.

CHAPTER 25

"I've got to call Ross," she said aloud. She reached for the phone and quickly dialed the pharmacy number.

Ross answered.

"Have you seen the morning paper yet?"

"No. Haven't had time. Why?"

"There's a huge front page headline and an extensive article about Birchwood Manor. They're under investigation by the state for some of the deaths that have occurred there during the past year. It seems a number of those who have died in the last year left generous gifts to a particular charity. A number of families have joined in the complaint."

Ross let out a long, low whistle.

Maggie continued. "The charges by families are that they felt their family members may have been brainwashed after living at Birchwood Manor for a few months. The article said that one of their residents started talking to their family about a wonderful charity specifically geared to elderly folks called *Safe Keepers*. The person told their family that they had provided for the charity in their will. When this particular man died quite suddenly of a heart attack, and his will was read, he had left over half of his estate to this charity. The large amount came as quite a shock to the family.

"The man's daughter went to visit a friend of her father's who also lived at Birchwood Manor. She asked him if he'd heard of this charity. He told her he had. When she asked if he was donating to it, he told her absolutely not. She asked him why, and he told her, 'Because I don't want to die. And I don't want to talk about it anymore, so please don't ask me. And don't mention my name to anyone, don't tell them about this conversation. I just keep my mouth shut and stay out of trouble.'

"This upset the daughter terribly, and she could tell her father's friend was frightened. She contacted several family members of residents who had died in the past year and found that their loved ones had also left generous gifts to this same charity in their wills. Some had lived for a few weeks after changing their wills, some had lived for months.

"A group of them met with an attorney. He began uncovering some disturbing facts. To make a long story short, it was discovered that this charity was created and administrated by the Andersons and could be traced to some off-shore accounts. So it definitely appeared to be benefiting them.

"Now these families are demanding a full investigation into their loved ones' deaths. The bodies of the deceased are going to be exhumed! They must have thought I was a part of that, and that's why they acted so strangely when I was there. They're running scared. And it sounds like it's with good reason!"

"But why didn't she want to answer your questions about Tom when she learned that's why you were there?"

"I don't know. Perhaps he's involved in it, too. The neighbor did say that he seemed to be in a hurry to leave from his last visit."

"Could be," Ross said. "Or maybe he was running late to catch a plane and we're reading something into his departure that isn't there."

The Harringtons continued to follow the Birchwood Manor story in the newspaper and on the local news. Not much new came to light in the next few days.

On Tuesday evening, Melanie phoned to say the paralegal from her attorney's office had the papers ready for everyone to sign. She was willing to see them on Wednesday afternoon since that was Ross's day off.

Maggie made arrangements to have the Kellers watch the children. They didn't mention where they were going as they didn't want Keri to be disappointed at being left behind.

She was talking less and less about her mother these days and Maggie viewed it with very mixed feelings. She was glad Keri was happy here and was adjusting so well to her busy, new life. She loved them all, and they loved her. When Melanie did die, this would make it a little easier for Keri though she would be very sad at the loss. And still, Maggie was saddened that the little girl was growing away from her mother, saddened that it had become a necessity for them to be apart. Just when Melanie had changed her former ways and found a real love and purpose in her life, she had been stricken by this cruel, incurable illness.

...

Wednesday

Hillary Lane, the paralegal, was already at Melanie's when Maggie and Ross arrived.

After the reading through of the paperwork and signing was completed she said, "I hope you realize this is just the first step. Sometimes this process can take months. I think it's wise that you've also added an addendum to your will stating your wishes for your daughter. The other potential problem that could slow this process is if the child's father should show up and try to block the adoption."

"The father is listed as unknown on the birth certificate. I don't think there's any chance of that happening. I don't think her birth father even knows he fathered her," Melanie was quick to say.

"Well," Ms. Lane said, "we'll get the process underway and hope it doesn't take too long." She offered Melanie her hand. "You're a brave woman and a very loving mother," she said.

Her voice betrayed the emotion she was feeling. "It's nice to meet you, too, Mr. and Mrs. Harrington. You're all very special people."

Maggie walked to the door with her then returned to the living room in time to hear Ross say, "Have you given anymore thought as to how you want to handle this with Keri?"

CHAPTER 26

As Maggie looked into Melanie's eyes it struck her how much more frail she appeared now than when they arrived. Signing the papers had taken a heavy toll on her. Maggie sat down by Ross and waited for Melanie's response.

It was a moment in coming. Finally she shook her head, "I've thought of little else. And I'm still not sure how I want to handle this. I waiver between us telling her together, and she and I talking about it alone."

Ross nodded. "I understand how you feel. I'm sure this is the hardest situation you've ever faced. We'll do it however you want, but Melanie, I personally think it should begin as something between just you and Keri. We won't be far away, just not there with you. I think it will be a special time between mother and daughter, to let her know you've done this because she's so dear to you, and you want her to be with a family who wants her very much and loves her very much. As she grows older, the memory of it will be very special to her."

Melanie let out a little sob. "Ross, you're a gem. How could I have been such a fool? And Maggie, you're wonderful too. You're two lucky people, and I thank God you've been such a support to me and so wonderful and loving with Keri."

There was a knock on the door. Ross went to answer it. It was the Hospice nurse. Before leaving, Maggie and Ross made arrangements to bring Keri back on the weekend. Driving home, Maggie said, "What an emotional afternoon. I feel spent. I can only imagine how poor Melanie feels. I hope and pray that she lasts until Saturday. She looked so awfully fragile this afternoon."

The next day was Thursday. Ross and Maggie kept their afternoon appointment to meet their new attorney, John Barrow.

He was a large man, rather laid back and very pleasant. This immediately put Maggie at ease. Though she'd been eager for the meeting, she'd also been apprehensive about it. She felt uneasy about anything in which Michael was involved.

When the appointment ended and they rose to leave, Ross and John shook hands. Then the attorney reached for Maggie's hand and said, "With what you've told me today, I don't think you have anything to worry about. The facts about Dr. Kerns are down in black and white. They can be substantiated and that's pretty hard to argue with. He's exhibited some mighty bizarre behavior. I think under the circumstances the judge is going to be sympathetic to what you can prove about him. Of course, we'll watch the court schedule and ask for delays until we know we have the right sitting judge if necessary."

"I feel so much better since meeting with you. Thank you," Maggie said.

"Now you do know that they've requested DNA testing to prove paternity, right?"

"I understand that. I didn't want Michael to know that he was Tyler's father, but he inadvertently found out I was pregnant. And I haven't denied that he's the birth father. I just don't think he's fit to have contact with Tyler. My child knows only one real father, and that's Ross. They adore one another. It would be traumatic to bring another father into our son's life now, and I'll do anything I can to prevent it. And Michael has exhibited such bizarre behavior at times. He also has such bad addictions." Maggie knew her emotions were showing, that she was rambling, so she added. "I prefer for Tyler not to have to go through the testing. But, of course, I'll comply if the court orders it."

"They will. Take my word for it," Mr. Barrow assured her. "You may as well set up the appointment. Duke is a good place to have it done."

Ross noticed a picture of a modified NASCAR racing car on John Barrow's desk as he rose. "You a racing fan?"

"A fan and a driver," John replied. "That's my car, number 55. Did a lot of racing at Bowman Gray Stadium." He lifted the picture and handed it to Ross. "How about you? You a fan?"

"Very nice," Ross replied, as he studied the photo. "Chevy Cavalier, isn't it? I took in a few races in my younger days."

"Yep, she's sleek and fast too. Six-hundred-plus horsepower."

Before the Harrington's left, the attorney's paralegal, Shelly, scheduled another appointment for the following week. Maggie felt extremely hopeful as they drove back to Serenity. She hoped she wasn't being overly optimistic.

When they reached the house, there was a message on the answering machine. Maggie listened. She called to Ross. When he joined her, she punched in the replay code, and handed him the receiver. She stood at his side feeling shaken.

CHAPTER 27

Ross dialed the number the woman left. He put the phone on speaker so Maggie could hear too. The call was answered by the Hospice operator.

Ross identified himself and asked for Nan Hancock. He didn't have to wait long.

"Mr. Harrington. Thank you for returning my call. I'm sorry to have to tell you that Melanie Harrington passed away at home late this afternoon. I was there with her. She and I had talked briefly about her wishes when she was gone. Then she just closed her eyes and slipped away."

Maggie felt tears sting her eyes as she listened. She had been afraid that was what the call would be when the Hospice nurse asked them to call her.

"I'm glad she wasn't alone," Ross said into the receiver. "And I'm glad she didn't struggle."

The nurse continued. "She left some papers for you. I have them with me. And she told me she had made all of the arrangements for her funeral. She was a very organized woman and quite a brave one."

"She was. Thank you," Ross said softly. "Perhaps we can meet with you and get the papers when we come for her funeral."

"Oh. One more thing. There's a large envelope from Mrs. Harrington for her little girl."

They spoke for a few more minutes making arrangements to get together before they said good-bye.

When he broke the connection, Maggie leaned against her husband. "I feel so terribly sad," she said. Her voice was barely above a whisper.

Ross took her in his arms and held her tightly. "I know. I feel the same. And Maggie, I want you to know that I love you so much. I'm so blessed to have you in my life." He pulled her even closer and kissed her forehead.

"I guess it's going to be up to us to tell Keri now."

"Yes. But not tonight, Darling. Why don't we get a good night's rest before we face that?"

"You're right, Ross. And we don't want to tell her before her bedtime. In fact, maybe we should wait until we get the papers Melanie left and the letter for Keri before we say anything. It'll only be a couple more days."

"I think that might be a good idea. Let's see how we feel about it in the morning. In the meantime, why don't you call Caroline and see if she'd like to keep the children overnight. I think we need this evening to ourselves."

"I agree." Maggie stepped away from her husband and reached for the phone. When Caroline answered, she posed the question.

"We'd love to keep them over night. Hold on a minute, honey. I'll see what they say."

Maggie heard excited squeals in the background. "I heard. I'll see you mid-morning and thanks."

"No. Thank you," Caroline said with a little chuckle.

Ross left her to go to the freezer to get something out for dinner. Maggie stayed behind for a moment reflecting on what a happy, changed woman Caroline was from the time Maggie first arrived in Serenity. Caroline had been deeply depressed from the loss of their only child, Joy, also a nurse. She had given up on life, turned inward pulling her grief in around her, shutting out everyone who loved her. Slowly, Maggie had become like a second adopted daughter to her and now, first

Tyler and then Keri became a part of her world. Caroline's life had taken on new meaning. Maggie whispered a short prayer of thanks and walked to the kitchen to join her husband.

"I got a couple of steaks out of the freezer. I'll stick them in the microwave to thaw. How does that sound?"

"Sounds good for you. But I think I'd rather have one of the hamburger patties from Omaha Steaks."

He looked at her and smiled then exchanged her steak for the patty.

"I'll scrub a couple of potatoes and stick them in the microwave in a few minutes," she said. "In the meantime, I'll throw a tossed salad together."

...

When the dishes were in the dishwasher, Ross poured them each a glass of wine. "Would you like to drink this out on the swing? It's still nice out there."

"Yes. I'd like that." Maggie picked up a sweater from the hall tree and slipped it around her shoulders. They went out onto the porch and sat down on the swing. She had to slip the sweater off after only a few minutes.

It was unseasonably warm for an early spring evening. Jonquils and buttercups were already in bloom. Maggie's pansies had survived the relatively mind winter. Soon their yard would be a blaze of color and the air fragrant with the scent of hundreds of blossoms. This was Maggie's favorite time of year. She took a sip of her wine and breathed in the fresh spring air before turning toward Ross.

"Would you like to walk to the water's edge?"

He nodded, rose and reached for her hand. They headed for the little bridge he had built several years ago. It had kept him occupied during those difficult days right after Melanie left him for another man. Now they were mourning her loss in an entirely different way. And he no longer felt any animosity toward her. Only sadness for her because she had died so young, and heartbreak for the little girl she had left behind.

"Are you thinking about Melanie?" Maggie asked.

"I am."

"Me too."

Ross looked down at her. "We've had so much to deal with recently, let's put it all to rest for a little while. Let's be selfish. Let's think only of us tonight, Maggie. Just you and me, and no one else."

He pulled her into an embrace and kissed her with such intensity that she fell against him. He eased her onto the soft green grass at the water's edge. His lips never left hers as he lowered himself over her. "You're the world to me, Maggie...my everything," he whispered, his voice husky with passion. Tenderly his hand found her thigh beneath her denim skirt and caressed it, slowly moving upward. The sun had set. Dusk enveloped them. The Caroloina moon glowed dimly through tissue paper clouds.

The soothing sounds of the balmy country night began to serenade them softly as they made love beneath a budding maple tree in the privacy of their own little paradise. Tonight they truly had shut the world out; it was just the two of them, only Ross and Maggie.

...

When they returned from Melanie's funeral, they were ready to talk to Keri. Mrs. Hancock, the Hospice nurse had come to the service and she brought with her a briefcase with a number of papers Melanie had left for them. As Maggie looked through the various envelopes during the drive back, she came to the large brown envelope with Keri's name on it. It was labeled to be opened by Ross and Maggie Harrington. Inside were several sealed white letter size envelopes each addressed to Keri at different ages.

"Ross, look. She's left Keri a number of letters. Here's one for now. Shall I open it or would you like to?"

"You do it, honey. You can read it to me."

Maggie broke the seal and began to read. It brought tears to her eyes. She read it to herself first before trying to read it aloud.

CHAPTER 28

Maggie woke before Ross on Sunday morning and had the coffee brewed when he joined her. After Breakfast they planned to read Melanie's letter to Keri. They would turn on cartoons for Tyler and this would give them some time alone with Keri. Later they would all go to church.

Ross went to get the Saturday paper out of the mail box while Maggie poured their coffee. There was another article about Birchwood Manor on the front page. As they sipped their coffee, he read it aloud. It was basically a recap of what the previous articles had said, and the facility was still being allowed to operate while the investigation continued.

"That really surprises me," Maggie said. "I'd have expected the state to close it down as soon as it came under scrutiny."

"As the article says, they have passed all state inspections with flying colors, and they're still just allegations until the bodies are exhumed and the autopsy results are in."

"I know," she agreed. "And there are no charges of abuse from any of the residents there…unless they're too frightened to complain to anyone. But I'd be willing to bet they won't have any new admissions until the results are in."

"I wouldn't bet against you on that one," Ross said with a chuckle.

Maggie listened. "I think I hear Tyler. I'll go up and check on him." As she started out of the kitchen, Keri wandered in wearing her favorite long sleeved pink flannel nightgown, rubbing her eyes. Maggie stooped down, hugged her tightly and kissed her before continuing on to Tyler's room.

...

After a breakfast of the children's favorites, French toast, sugar and syrup, and chocolate milk, Maggie turned on the cartoons for Tyler and favorite stuffed dog, Puppy. "Mommy and Daddy will be out on the porch with Keri," she told him. "If you need me, call me. Okay, honey?"

He grinned at her. "All by myself? Yeah! I'm big boy. I won't need you." He snuggled against Puppy on the floor to watch TV feeling very grown up.

It sent a little pang through Maggie as she kissed him. She left the room and joined Ross and Keri who were already out on the porch sitting on the swing.

They sat for a few minutes as Keri talked about how much she loved boating with Ross and Tyler. She told them it was one of her favorite things about being here. Then she spoke of wanting to take her mother in the boat the next time she came. That gave Maggie the perfect opening. She glanced in through the window and was relieved to see that Tyler had fallen asleep with his head on Puppy.

"Keri," she began, "You know your mommy has been very sick, don't you?"

She looked at Maggie with childish innocence. "Yes, she has. Is she all better now?"

Maggie felt a little pang of acid shoot through her stomach. She looked at Ross.

"I'm afraid not, honey. Your mommy sent a letter to tell you about it. Maggie has it for you."

Keri's eyes lit up, and she clapped her little hands together. "I can't read very many words," she said.

"I know," Maggie said softly. "This is a letter that she wanted me to read to you."

Keri nodded. "Okay." She watched intently as Maggie pulled the envelope from her pocket and removed the letter. As she did, Maggie prayed that they were handling this right, the way Melanie would have wanted. She began to read softly and slowly.

"My precious Keri, I love you sooo much. I know that you understand that Mommy has been very sick. That is why you went to stay with Ross and Maggie and Tyler, because I was too sick to take care of you. I have been talking to God a lot, and I asked Him to help me feel better. He told me the only way He could do that was to take me away from our home on earth and bring me to His home in Heaven. I asked Him, 'How will Keri know that I still love her, and that I'm watching over her always even though we can't see each other or touch each other anymore?' God said 'This is what I will do.'' He told me He would put a star in the sky that Keri could look at every night, and that star would be me watching over you. He said that no matter where you went, if you looked up, the star would be there and you would know that I love you. You and I always loved playing Hide and Seek, so God said that even on nights that are cloudy and you can't see the star, it would still be there because on those nights, we would be playing our favorite game together and pretty soon you'd find me again. He also told me sometimes He'd send soft breezes that would be me hugging you and little drops of rain would be mommy kissing you.

I'm so proud of what a good girl you are. I want you to be happy and love Ross and Maggie and Tyler. And always know that I love you forever and ever and ever.

Hugs and kisses,
Mommy

Maggie read it without her voice breaking, because she had practiced it six times on Saturday evening before she went to bed. She read it once again early this morning while she waited for Ross to join her for coffee. She knew she had to be strong for Keri, and she had been.

There was silence for a moment. Then Ross said, "Keri, sweetheart, do you understand what your mommy was telling you in the letter?"

The child looked solemnly from one to the other of them. She remained silent for a moment. Ross and Maggie both waited for her response.

CHAPTER 29

"That Mommy went away to Heaven?" Her voice was tiny, barely audible.

"Yes, that's what it means." Ross said quietly, lifting Keri onto his lap. "I'm so sorry, honey. Your mommy didn't want to leave you. She fought so hard to stay with you because she loves you so very much. But God wanted her to come home to Him, and He knew how much we all love you, and need you, so He took your mommy to His home so she wouldn't hurt anymore."

Keri's breath caught in her throat as tears clouded her blue eyes. She leaned against Ross and buried her face in his chest. She sobbed brokenheartedly. Ross cradled her in his strong arms and began to swing ever so lightly. Maggie moved over and took the seat next to her husband and patted the child's back tenderly. They said nothing, letting her cry, knowing she needed to let her tears flow.

At one point, Maggie turned and peered through the window at Tyler. He was still napping on Puppy.

...

Maggie was glad to see the sun shining brightly on Monday morning. Sunday had been such a bleak, emotionally draining day. They had all gone to church Sunday morning. Keri was very clingy. She wanted to sit on Maggie's lap all through the church service. Maggie kept her arms wrapped about the child throughout. Tyler hopped back and forth from his father's lap to Caroline's to Charlie's, completely oblivious to what had transpired earlier that morning.

Sunday afternoon had turned gloomy and began to drizzle. Keri ran out into the yard to catch her mother's kisses. Melanie's letter had truly been a God-send. Keri carried it in her pocket all day along with some pictures of the two of them her mother had sent along in the letter.

After breakfast on Monday, Maggie planned to take the children to playschool and stay with them, even though it wasn't her day to volunteer. She felt their lives should continue as normally as possible, but she wanted to stay close to Keri, and to Tyler, for their sake and her own. Time together had become even more precious to her in these last several days.

While she was at the church playschool, she phoned Lindsay. Maggie felt she had abandoned her friend recently, and she needed support now too.

Lindsay was pleased to hear Maggie's voice. They made arrangements to get together during Lindsay's lunch hour. She would come to the church.

When she arrived, much to the delight of all six children in attendance, she had Happy Meals for each of them and lunch for the adults as well.

"What a sweet thing for you to do, Lindsay. You know how to score with the little ones."

"I love kids," she said, appearing a little embarrassed at the kind words.

"How are you doing? Did you talk to Caroline and Charlie yet?"

"I did. And they were terrific, just like you said they'd be. Actually, Caroline seemed pleased but terribly angry at Tom. I got the feeling she didn't like Tom even though she had never met him. Anyway, to make a long story short, I'm going to stay on in Serenity, at least for the time being. It's more home to me than anyplace I've lived except Montana."

Dixie Land

Maggie nodded and embraced her. "I'm so glad! I know you've made the right decision."

"Now," Lindsay said, "tell me about Melanie. I know you've really had it rough these past few days."

Maggie filled her in and told her how bravely Keri had taken the news. She ended with the new evening ritual they had begun of going out onto the porch, finding Melanie's star and blowing kisses to it.

After Keri finished her Happy Meal, she ran to Maggie and hugged her. Tyler was at her heels. Keri had done it several times earlier today and, each time she did, Maggie kissed her and told her she loved her. And whenever Keri ran to Maggie, Tyler came along behind her, reaching his little arms up and puckering his lips as he said, "Me too!" Afterward, they would run back to their play.

Lindsay chuckled at their antics as she glanced at her watch. "Gotta go. Don't worry about me. I'm going to be fine, Maggie. I've quit feeling sorry for myself."

"Good for you. Of course, you'll be fine. I'm so glad you're staying."

...

The week flew by. Maggie went to playschool each day with the children. On Thursday, the Kellers watched them while Maggie and Ross met with John Barrow. As their appointment was drawing to a close, Shelly, his paralegal knocked on the conference room door. "Excuse me. I just got a confirmation of our court date. Next Tuesday morning in Raleigh."

John looked up from his paperwork. "Who's on the bench?"

"Judge Madeline Chamberlain." Shelly stepped out and closed the door behind her.

John appeared thoughtful as he stroked his chin. He nodded. "That's okay. She can be tough, but she's fair. We could do much worse. We should be okay with her."

By the way the attorney said it, Maggie wondered if he was really that confident or trying to convince himself and put their minds at ease.

CHAPTER 30

Maggie and Ross discussed driving to Raleigh on Monday night so they wouldn't feel rushed for their court date Tuesday morning, but both agreed they didn't want to leave Keri overnight so soon after the loss of her mother. Instead, Caroline and Charlie slept at the Harrington's to allow the children to sleep later the next morning and Maggie and Ross rose at 5:00 a.m. and drove to Raleigh.

Maggie was so nervous; she had barely slept all night. She got out of bed before the alarm went off and took her shower. She studied herself in the bathroom mirror. She had circles under her eyes and they looked puffy and she so wanted to appear rested, calm and in control. She didn't, for even one second, want Michael to think this had unnerved her, though it clearly had. And, how she dreaded seeing him again. Thank God, she had a wonderful man like Ross at her side. He would be her rock. He appeared to have slept well and he was taking the hearing much more in stride than she was. She pulled out her vanity drawer and took out a tube of Preparation-H gel, removed the cap and dabbed a little beneath each eye and smoothed it in. Some of the puffiness receded immediately.

She was downstairs in the kitchen when Ross joined her looking handsome and rested. She scrambled some eggs for him but drank only half of her coffee. Her stomach was too unsettled to put anything more in it. Perhaps she'd feel more like eating at lunch time. Maybe by then her initial jitters would have abated somewhat; she certainly hoped so.

They arrived at the courthouse with thirty minutes to spare, found a parking place in the parking deck and waited another fifteen minutes before heading for the building. They were scheduled to meet in the judge's chambers.

They had quite a long walk but Maggie was glad. The exercise calmed her, but only slightly. When they reached the room and stepped inside, John Barrow and his assistant, Shelly, were already there.

"Good. We have a few minutes to spare. I always like to be early." he said.

Maggie glanced at her watch. They had eight minutes to wait. The "other side" hadn't shown up yet.

"Now don't you worry, Mrs. Harrington," John said. "We're going to come out of this just fine." He patted his leather briefcase. "I have everything we need in here."

The clock inside the judge's inner-office struck nine and still they were the only people there. "These things are often delayed," John said to Ross who appeared calm throughout the wait.

He nodded at the attorney.

Maggie felt that if something didn't happen in the next few minutes, she was going to scream. She began to hope that Michael wouldn't show up, that the judge would call them in and, with Michael missing, dismiss the case.

Two minutes later, the door of the waiting room opened and a stunning woman of perhaps forty, give or take a year or two, stepped into the room and removed her sunglasses. Her medium-length, silky-blond hair fell loosely about her face, and she wore tan slacks and a brown tweed blazer.

She nodded to them. "I'll be with you in a few minutes," she said before going into her inner-chamber.

"That," John Barrow announced quietly, "was Madeline Chamberlain." The door to the judge's chambers had no more than closed when the waiting room door opened again. In walked three men in business suits and one woman. The last to enter was Michael Kerns.

Maggie's heart sank. He did show up! And it appeared he had quite a support team. Were they all legal representatives or were they character witnesses and if so, what kind of lies were they going to spring on the judge?

And the judge was a beautiful woman...Michael's specialty.

CHAPTER 31

Before the new arrivals had a chance to sit, everyone was called into the judge's chambers. John Barrow, Maggie and Ross took seats on one side of the massive rectangular mahogany conference table, Michael's entourage sat opposite them.

Michael caught Maggie's eye and flashed her a warm smile. He partially rose from his chair and extended his right hand across the table to Ross. Introductions followed. Michael smiled and nodded at Judge Chamberlain, as their eyes met.

This is Michael at his best. Maggie thought. *Oozing with the little boy innocence and charm that was his trademark whenever he was trying to win someone over.*

The judge hadn't bothered to don her legal robe. There were several folders on her desk. She lifted then rearranged them. She stacked them in a neat pile before laying them down again and opening the one on top. She spoke to the gathering briefly, admonishing everyone to keep the hearing civil and courteous.

They began the business at hand. As Michael's attorney started to speak, Maggie's heart rate accelerated. In his opening discourse he briefly touched on the tribulations Michael had faced in the last two and a half years. His main focus was Michael's courage and desire to change, his successful recovery and his deep desire to play an active role in his son's life. Throughout the attorney's speech, Michael sat calmly, affirming the words with a nod periodically. The judge listened intently.

Kevin was right, he's good, Maggie thought. *If I didn't know Michael so well, he'd have me feeling sorry for him. I really don't like this.* But she too listened closely and showed no reaction to anything that was said.

One of the men and the woman with Michael were character witnesses. They made Michael sound like a candidate for sainthood. Maggie thought they went overboard. She hoped the judge agreed with her. Maggie studied Madeline Chamberlain as she listened to the woman praise Michael. Her expression gave no clue as to what she was thinking.

They broke for lunch and returned to the judge's chambers an hour and a half later.

Then it was John Barrow's turn. He took a moment to lift his briefcase onto the table and removed several folders from it. Then he began in a deep, resonant voice. He went into much more detail about Michael's problems than his attorney had. Maggie was glad they didn't begin. Hopefully this more negative view of Michael would leave the lasting impression.

Mr. Barrow began with Maggie finding her then fiancé, Michael, in bed with her best friend, his admitted addictions to alcohol and gambling, his problems with the government, his uninvited attendance at Ross and Maggie's wedding where he wielded a gun, was arrested and taken out of the church in handcuffs. He gave places and dates for Michael's several admissions to rehab, his return to employment in a hospital and subsequent dismissal.

Judge Chamberlain listened just as intently to John Barrow's presentation as he had to Michael's attorney.

Michael showed no reaction to Maggie's attorney's disclosures. He appeared calm and confident.

At the end of the day, Judge Chamberlain offered Maggie and Michael an opportunity to add to what had been said previously. Both accepted. Michael deferred to Maggie. She reached for Ross's hand as she began.

"I feel the most important person in all of this is Tyler. From his birth, he's been in a loving, stable home. He knows only one father." She looked at her husband before continuing. "Ross married me knowing full well he was not Tyler's father. He's devoted to Tyler and our son adores him. He is the only father Tyler has ever known. In the past few weeks, our lives have taken on a sudden change. We are in the process of adopting a little girl whose mother died recently from lung cancer. Though Tyler has been very accepting of our new family member, I feel that currently, this is enough for him to cope with." Maggie took a sip of water before continuing. "Michael has had many problems, and I applaud his desire to heal himself, to seek help for his addictions. But I feel it is too soon to pronounce him cured.

"When we love someone truly, we want what is best for them, even if it isn't the way we personally want things to be. We all have to love Tyler enough to want what's the very best for him. And right now, that is staying within the only family structure he has ever known and welcoming his new 'little sister,' into his world." Maggie shifted her attention to Michael. "If you are truly concerned for Tyler as you profess to be, you should want what is best for him now too." She returned her attention to Judge Chamberlain. "Thank you, your Honor."

"Thank you, Mrs. Harrington." The judge looked at Michael and nodded. "Dr. Kerns, we'll hear from you now."

"I thank you, too, your Honor. I can't disagree with what Maggie has just said. "Though I don't know Tyler as Ross does, he is my blood. And I want to accept my responsibility toward him. I want to know him as Ross does. I've made some terribly foolish mistakes in my life. I would give anything if they had never happened. I loved this woman dearly," he looked at Maggie. "I was a fool to do what I did to her. I went to her and tried to win her back but she wouldn't give me another chance." He looked at Maggie solemnly and then at the judge. "I can't blame her though. I hurt her terribly, broke her trust when she was at her lowest. But I've sought treatment because I knew I was ill. And I have changed. All I'm asking of the court is that I have a chance to know my son and show him the love I feel for him. I'd be willing to start slowly, keeping his best interest always in mind." Michael cleared his throat. "That's all I have to say.

"Thank you, Dr. Kerns." Madeline Chamberlain looked solemn as she glanced from Maggie to Michael then looked down at the open folder before her.

CHAPTER 32

Madeline Chamberlain wrote something in the file and closed the folder. She glanced at her watch. "It's late. I'm going to ask you to return tomorrow morning at 10:00 a.m. I'll announce my decision then."

...

"Another night to worry," Maggie said as their car headed down the highway toward home. "I wish I could read her. She shows absolutely no reaction to anything."

"You're right about that," Ross agreed. "I watched her closely when everyone was having their say. She's a poker player, a real pro."

When they reached the house, they found Lil there visiting with Caroline and Charlie. After greeting the children who were watching a DVD about penguins, Maggie and Ross joined the adults in the kitchen.

"What a nice surprise, Lil," Maggie said.

"I couldn't wait to hear what happened today."

Everyone looked at Maggie in anticipation. "Nothing. Nothing was decided. We have to go back tomorrow morning."

"Do you think it'll be over tomorrow?" Caroline asked.

"I certainly hope so. She filled them in on their day while Ross poured everyone a glass of wine.

"None for me," Lil said. "I have to drive back to town tonight. One glass and I'd be ready to nap on the couch. That drug store is going to open again tomorrow morning, and I need to be there early. I have some supplies to put up."

"We'll be glad to stay over again if you'd like," Caroline said.

"That'd be great," Ross said. He handed Caroline and then Charlie their wine. Then there's no reason you can't drink this, is there?"

Charlie chuckled. "None I can think of," he said.

When Maggie concluded her wrap-up of the day, Lil stood. "Well, good luck, Maggie, Ross." She went into the living room and picked her sweater up from the back of the sofa. She returned to the kitchen to give Maggie a hug. "I'll head on back to town now. Call me as soon as you know something, okay?"

After Lil left, Caroline said, "I think our Lil has an admirer."

"Really? Who?" Maggie was curious.

"David Helms. She said they ate lunch together today. Fact is, he brought lunch into the pharmacy for the both of them."

Ross pulled a chair up to the table, "I've noticed he has a reason to come by about every other day lately. Always comes back to talk to Lil for a few minutes. I'm not surprised. After his wife Anna died, he was really broken up. Lil was very kind to him. She had such a hard time when Henry died. You know because of the circumstances, their quarrel and all, she kind of blamed herself. Anyway, I think David kind of leaned on Lil. And now I think he's beginning to like the idea of having her to spend time with. Lil's good company. And we all know, she's quite a little character."

"She is," Caroline agreed. She really reached out to me after Joy died. I just wasn't very receptive for a long time there. I made it pretty rough on Charlie, too." She reached over and placed her hand on his. "Wasted years," she said. "I appreciate Lil and all of you."

"I know this sounds like a canonizing ceremony for Lil, but she was wonderful to me, too," Maggie added. "From the day I arrived in Serenity, she was so accepting of me. She looked out for me and mothered me, just like you and Charlie did."

After dinner the men went into the living room to watch TV. Maggie and Caroline cleaned up the kitchen, then took the children upstairs for their baths. After the bedtime ritual with Tyler and Keri, the adults sat in the front room and visited for a few minutes.

Maggie stretched and yawned. "I've got to try to get some sleep. I barely got any last night."

"I'll second that," Charlie said. "I slept fine, but I'm tired just the same."

...

Everyone was on time for the 10:00 a.m. appointment with Judge Chamberlain. Again, she wore no judicial robe. Today she had dressed in a Carolina Blue pants suit which looked stunning with her silky golden tresses and sapphire blue eyes. Michael seemed to be having a hard time keeping his eyes off of her.

As soon as everyone was seated, she began. "I asked you to come back today as I wanted to reflect on my decision. I don't like making hasty decisions on matters of grave importance. A child's welfare **is** a matter of grave importance to me."

Maggie felt nervous. Last night, she had slept poorly again, and when she had dosed off, she'd had fretful dreams of Tyler and Michael and not being able to find her child. She prayed silently as she tried to concentrate on what the judge was saying.

"I listened with great interest," Judge Chamberlain continued, "to what each side had to say yesterday. When parents are not together, it's always a no win situation for the children of the union. They are the ones who are cheated. That is always sad to me. I sympathize with Mrs. Harrington who is trying to provide a secure, stable environment for her son, who at a very young age is experiencing some unsettling circumstances in his life with the sudden addition of a new sibling. I admire the

Harringtons for agreeing to bring a child who desperately needs a loving family into their home. I spent some time last night looking into the circumstances of how this came about. I feel they are very sincere in their desire to make this as natural and easy for Tyler and their adopted daughter as they possibly can."

Maggie felt her spirits rise a little.

"I also understand Dr. Kerns' desire to know this little boy he has fathered. Sadly in this country, we are seeing too many fathers who are not accepting responsibility for their children. I applaud Dr. Kerns' efforts to seek treatment for his addictions, his desire to heal himself and play a responsible role in his young son's life. I realize that the earlier he enters the boy's life, the easier it will be for Tyler to accept Dr. Kerns into his world."

Maggie's heart raced. *Oh, dear God, she's going to grant Michael what he's asked for.* She felt sick. She reached for Ross's hand.

Maggie became aware of Judge Chamberlain's voice again as she heard her say, "I pondered this case at great length last night. I did not arrive at this decision lightly."

CHAPTER 33

"At this time, I'm going to deny Dr. Kern's request for joint-custody of Tyler. I agree with Mrs. Harrington. Time has not been sufficient to feel with any certainly that there will not be a relapse for Dr. Kerns." She turned her attention to Michael. "In two- and-a-half years, you have had three brief hospitalizations. If I were to grant your wishes, and you found the need to seek treatment again, that could be traumatic for Tyler. He has enough adjusting to do currently. I would be willing to revisit your request a year from now if you continue on your road to recovery."

Maggie felt relief wash over her. For the first time since this all began, she felt her muscles relax. As she looked at Michael she saw the square line of his tightly clenched jaw. He was angry...things had not gone as he expected them to. The judge may not realize it but Maggie knew.

"Judge Chamberlain," he began, in a well modulated voice. "I'd like to say that I'm deeply disappointed. I do understand your reasoning. I must accept your ruling. I still want to know my son." His jaw was no longer tight, he wore his 'imploring little boy look,' as he addressed the judge.

"I'm not finished," Madeline Chamberlain said. "I'm not granting joint custody at this time. I will, however, grant visitation rights as long as Mrs. Harrington and her husband are both present. You may work out the arrangements yourselves as to how you wish to handle the visits."

Michael looked across at Maggie, with slightly raised eyebrows and smiled. She felt a terrible pang of anguish wash through her. They would have to put up with Michael after all. How could this be happening when all she wanted was to have him out of their lives once and for all? She found it really hard to believe that Michael desperately wanted to know Tyler. Knowing him as she did, she felt this was all about his winning. She read his smile as having made the first inroads toward legally intruding himself into their family. And there wasn't a thing she and Ross could do about it. It was court ordered.

As Maggie and Ross headed for the parking deck, Michael called to them. "Wait. Let's talk for a minute," he said as he reached them.

Why couldn't we have been just a little faster getting away? Maggie wondered.

"Look," Michael began. "I understand how you feel...I can't say that I blame you, but I have changed. I think it's important that we have a civil relationship, for Tyler's sake."

"I agree with that," Ross said. "Tyler's well-being is what's most important."

"So, when do you want to see him?" Maggie asked. "I don't want it to be in our home. I think the best place would be for us to meet you at a park somewhere. The weather's getting really nice now. We could spend a couple hours playing with the children. As you know, we have a little girl now, too."

"Yes, I heard that from you and the judge. That sounds like a good, natural place to meet. We can say we're old friends."

How about old acquaintances? Maggie thought, but she said. "I think that's a good idea. When do you want to have our first meeting?"

"I was thinking of..." Michael's cell phone rang interrupting them. He took it from his belt clip and looked at it. "I need to take this. Please excuse me." He stepped away from them and answered the call.

As he spoke, he distanced himself even further from them. Maggie watched him intently. Michael became agitated as the conversation continued.

CHAPTER 34

When Michael's call ended, he returned to them. His manner had changed abruptly. He looked strained and pale. "I'm sorry. Something urgent has come up. I'm going to have to call you to set up a time. Would you please give me your phone number?"

Ross removed one of his business cards from his wallet and handed it to Michael. "You can reach me here most days. And someone can always get a message to me if I'm not there."

Michael put the card in his pocket and left them abruptly.

"What do you make of that?" Maggie asked. "I'd give anything to know who that call was from and what it was about."

...

Maggie's week was busy and the week passed with no contact from Michael. On Friday, She invited the Kellers, Lil and Lindsay to come for dinner. It was a pleasant evening without any mention of Tom. Lindsay seemed to be adjusting to his absence in her life. When the meal was finished, they took their coffee into the living room.

Lil said, "I hear tell the Cassidy's son is moving back to Serenity. He's an accountant so it looks like we'll have a new business opening in town."

"I heard he might move back. Is it certain now?" Caroline asked.

Return to Serenity

"Megan down at the realty company said he was down looking for a place to buy." Lil said. "His dad's health has deteriorated so much this past year; he's really a handful for Martha to look after these days. It was either a nursing home or Adam move back home. Martha couldn't bear to put him in a nursing home so that's why."

"I'm sure this business with Birchwood Manor has put the fear of God into a lot of folks about nursing homes," Lindsay said.

"You're right about that," Lil agreed.

"That Adam sure was a good looking young man when he was in high school." Caroline said.

Lil continued, "Megan said he's a hunk of a man, tall, with a good build, auburn hair, and brown eyes. Said she wished she was twenty years younger. He's single, you know."

Charlie laughed. "What say we go outside and take a look at your garden, Ross? We'll leave these females to their gossip."

"Good idea." The men headed out through the kitchen to the backyard.

"So how old do you think he is?" Maggie asked.

"We'll, he went to school with Joy," Caroline said. "I think he was a year behind her, so he must be twenty-seven or twenty-eight."

Lil got a twinkle in her eye. "Sounds like about the right age for you, Lindsay. And such a nice family he comes from."

"I'm not looking for any involvements now."

"Lil's our eternal match-maker." Maggie said. "She had it in mind to get Ross and me together from the day I arrived in town. I have to admit, she was right. He's the best thing that ever happened to me."

"Speaking of match-making," Caroline said, "I hear you've got an admirer, Lil"

Lil's face and neck instantly flushed crimson. "David and I are friends, nothing more," she said a little too quickly. "He's been so lost since Anna died. I've just tried to be a kind ear for him to bend."

"I heard he's been in the pharmacy several times a week lately," Lindsay joined in. "One of Doc's patients told me your name comes up in his conversations quite frequently these days."

"Ross said he brought in lunch for you and him one day recently." Maggie said. "I'm happy for you, Lil. You're a good friend and you deserve a good friend."

When the men rejoined them a few minutes later, the topic of conversation changed. Everyone left by 10:00 p.m.

Ross asked, "Would you like a glass of wine out on the porch before we turn in?"

"I don't think so. You go ahead and pour one for yourself, and I'll keep you company. I'll wait for you on the swing."

Maggie had a few mornings where she felt a little queasy lately. If her period was late, she planned to make an appointment with Doc. She hadn't mentioned it to Ross yet because she felt it was a little premature to get his hopes up. They had so wanted a child of their own. Though now probably wasn't the best time with everything that was happening in their lives, but if she was pregnant, they would be thrilled.

And Maggie was pleased, yet curious that Michael hadn't been in touch. It had been more than two weeks since the custody hearing ended.

On Wednesday, the morning paper had another article about Birchwood Manor. The first of the bodies was to be exhumed the following week. Maggie wondered how the Andersons were dealing with all of this. The place was still open but a number of the residents had moved out of the facility and gone to other nursing homes. The paper said their census had been cut almost in half. It also said that no findings would be disclosed until all of the bodies had been exhumed and the testing on all was completed.

Maggie's phone rang and she reached for it. It was Lindsay. "Do you mind if I put you on speaker?" She asked. "I'm in the middle of…"

"Sure," Lindsay interrupted. "No problem. I couldn't wait to tell you. Tom called. He said he misses me. He made a mistake to give it another try with his wife. We talked for an hour. Oh, Maggie, I'm so happy!"

"Did you tell him about the baby?"

"Well, no. Not until we're together. I'll tell him when I see him. Gotta go now but couldn't wait to tell you. Bye." Lindsay broke the connection.

Maggie shook her head as she pressed the speaker button. "I'm not so sure, Lindsay. Not so sure at all. Why did he have to call now? Why didn't he just leave her alone? If he had, maybe Lil would have succeeded at her match making between Lindsay and Adam." Maggie didn't know anything about him, but if his parents were any indication, he was a good man. And, he was coming home to help his mother care for his father.

"That Tom!" Maggie said aloud. She shook her head again.

...

Time flew by. When her period was three weeks late, without mentioning it to Ross, Maggie called Doc's clinic and set up an appointment to see him on Tuesday morning. If the outcome was what she thought it would be, she'd feed the children early, fix a romantic candlelight dinner for Ross and tell him while they ate.

...

Maggie arranged to drop the children off at the Keller's. Charlie would take them to play school and Maggie would pick them up after the appointment. Caroline had been concerned when she learned Maggie was going to see Doc. Maggie assured her that she was fine and just having a check-up which she didn't consider untrue. But Ross must be the first one she told. They would probably wait to tell Tyler and Keri until she began to show. For them to have to wait from now until signs that the baby was a reality was too long for little ones.

Maggie felt a little twinge of excitement as she helped the children into the back seat of the car. Keri buckled herself in while Maggie fastened Tyler's seat-belt. Since Keri could do her own, he always wanted to try to fasten his too. Maggie watched and helped him get it snapped.

As Maggie backed away from her car and straightened up, her breath caught in her throat as a powerful arm encircled her waist and held her tightly. Looking down she could see pants legs and hiking boots. She struggled to free herself as a cloth was pressed over her mouth and nose. It was wet, and the odor was strong and sickening. She continued to struggle, but her attacker was much too powerful for her to overcome. She heard the children's terrified cries as she lapsed into unconsciousness.

CHAPTER 35

As Maggie's awareness returned, she wasn't sure how much time had passed. Her first impulse was to turn to the back seat to check on her children. She was sluggish…dizzy and groggy…her body was having trouble doing what her brain told it to. She strained her neck…the children…they were gone! And so were their seats!

She turned back in time to see a car in front of hers. Through blurred eyes, she saw a tall man walking toward her. He reached her car and pulled her door open. In an instant, a multitude of things became clear to her. Panic gripped her! "No! Please no!" she screamed, fearing what this might do to her unborn child if she was pregnant. The cloth came down hard over her nose and mouth again. She slumped silently in the car seat.

...

When Maggie and the children didn't show up at the Keller's, Charlie was disappointed. He'd had one eye on the window for the last twenty minutes.

"Maybe she was running late and decided to take them directly to play school," Caroline said. "Still, it's not like Maggie to do that without calling us to let us know."

"Why don't you call over to the church," Charlie said.

"Let's wait and give her a few more minutes."

Ten minutes passed and still no Maggie and children.

"That's it," Caroline said rising from the sofa and going to the telephone. As she reached it, the phone chirped loudly, startling her. She lifted the receiver. "Hello…oh hello, Kathryn…No, she hasn't shown up yet. I was just heading for the phone to call the church to see if she went directly there for some reason. I'll call the church, Kathryn. You call the house to see if she's there. We need to try her cell phone too, maybe she had car trouble."

Caroline turned to Charlie. "Kathryn said she's late for her appointment."

A few minutes later Caroline and Kathryn spoke again. Maggie hadn't shown up at playschool. Neither of them had any luck reaching her. Caroline called Ross at the pharmacy. "Does Maggie happen to be there?" She asked. She waited for his reply. "Oh, no reason, I just wondered." Charlie was pacing the floor when Caroline hung up.

"Why didn't you tell Ross she didn't show up, and we can't reach her?"

"I didn't want to worry him at this stage. We're probably just being overly concerned. Maggie might have forgotten her appointment."

"No, you know she's too responsible to do anything like that," Charlie said. "I'm going out there and check on her. Do you want to ride with me?"

"You go out to their place, I'll stay here in case she comes or calls. Keep your cell phone on, Charlie, and call me when you get there. I'll let you know if I hear from her."

A few minutes later, Charlie turned down the long, tree and shrub-lined, gravel road that led to the Harringtons'. Just before he reached the area where the incline began, he noticed a car pulled off the road. It was partially obscured by the dense brush. He stopped, got out and started toward it. He had only taken a couple of steps when he recognized it as Maggie's. As he hurried to reach it, he turned his left ankle on the rutty terrain.

He fell to the ground. When he tried to get up, he couldn't. The pain in his leg and ankle was excruciating. Concern rising in him for Maggie and the children, he dragged himself through the brambles. Branches scratched his skin and snagged his clothing. He pushed on. When he reached the car, he grabbed the door knob and pulled himself up on his good leg. He opened the unlocked door and peered about the car. The key was still in the ignition. Tyler and Keri's car seats were missing. His eyes made a visual sweep of the wooded area around him. There was no sign of Maggie or the children within his vision. He knew he couldn't crawl far enough to search the woods. He returned his attention to her car. The window on the passenger side of the front seat was partially rolled down. There was a terrible, pungent odor in the interior. Charlie's heart sank. "Oh, dear, God," he sobbed. "Something has happened to our Maggie and the babies."

His heart pounded as he dragged himself back through the dense growth of vegetation to reach his cell phone which he had left in the car. "Fool," he chided himself. "You should have had the sense to put the phone in your pocket."

He was driven by such alarm and concern for Maggie and her children, that he didn't even feel the pain as he struggled, on belly and elbows, to reach his car to summon help.

Finally at the car, he hoisted himself up into a sitting position behind the steering wheel and dialed Caroline. While he waited for her to answer, he struggled to catch his breath. 'Come on, answer, honey!" Then he prayed silently. *And please, God, let Caroline tell me she's heard from Maggie and the babies.* Sadly, he feared this prayer would not be answered.

CHAPTER 36

"No word here. What did you find, Charlie?" Caroline asked.

"It doesn't look good. I found her car down in the woods headed out of the driveway. Keys are in the car. The children's seats are gone. There's a terrible odor in the car, I don't know what it is. Sort of puts me in mind of the ether they used to use in the old days. I'm really worried about them. To make matters worse, I've fallen. I've hurt my leg and ankle."

"Oh, Charlie, no! Is it your bad leg? Can you walk?" She was talking so loudly that her voice carried throughout the car.

"Yep, the left one. I had to drag myself back to the car. I need Sheriff Barton to come now and check this out. I'm worried...something's terribly wrong. I feel it in my bones. I'm gonna drive up to the house and see what I find there. You need to call Ross. And I'll need someone to drive my car back to town. I suppose you better let Doc know I'll be coming by for some x-rays later on."

"I'll do all that. I'll make the calls and get a ride out there. I'll drive you to Docs."

Caroline felt shaky as she disconnected from Charlie and began making calls.

Charlie started his car and drove up to the house. His ankle was throbbing...becoming more swollen by the minute. It wasn't long before he heard sirens in the distance. They grew louder. Sheriff Barton's car drove up behind him, with lights flashing, followed by Serenity's other police car. Charlie heard horns honking and another siren blaring, but the sound stopped before reaching the house. He opened his door, raised himself to a standing position and, balancing on one leg, held on to his car. Ross and Caroline arrived seconds later.

Sheriff Barton's voice boomed, "I sent for the firefighters because Caroline said you mentioned a foul odor. They're down checking out the car. Didn't want to take any chances on an explosion."

Ross got out of his car and raced to the house.

Caroline hurried to Charlie. "Oh look at you. You're all bruised and scratched. And your leg! You need to get off of it." Her voice was shaky.

Ross returned to them, his face ashen. "No sign of them inside and no signs of a struggle," He said. "Just no Maggie, Tyler and Keri." He looked as frantic as he sounded.

Caroline left Charlie and stepped to his side. She put her arm around his waist as the fire truck pulled into the yard.

One of the volunteers got out. He approached Sheriff Barton and the gathering. "I'm pretty sure that odor in the car is ether. We searched the woods around the area. No tire tracks, no sign of anyone or the kid's seats. No footprints beyond that car either. There are some large shoe tracks for a good sized area all around the car leading forward. A number of them are pretty badly smudged up indicating several trips back and forth. Whoever parked in front of Maggie's car. From the tracks, it was probably a full sized passenger car."

"Thanks, Josh," the sheriff said. "It looks like an abduction to me. We'd better get organized and start a search. I'll call the office and get the ball rolling with contacting the media, highway patrol, all the channels...if only we just knew what vehicle we were looking for. Maybe we can get a read on the tires."

"Count on us for any help you need!" Josh said.

Dixie Land

Ross felt sick. "Damn!" He said, through clenched teeth. "I should have stayed home today!" He looked at Caroline. "And when you called me asking if Maggie was at the pharmacy, you should have told me she was missing. We could have come out right then and maybe stopped this thing."

"Ross, I'm sorry. We didn't know anything was wrong at that point. Just that she was late, and with little ones, sometimes mothers run late."

"Ross, get a hold of yourself, man" Barton said. "We all know how bad this is for you. But placing blame isn't doing anyone any good. We all have to pull together."

Ross looked down and nodded. "I know. You're right. I'm sorry, Caroline," He turned to look into her sad, stricken eyes. "I know how much you both love them all. That was unfair of me...I'm just so damn worried and frustrated."

Caroline embraced Ross again. Tears began rolling down her cheeks. "I know, Ross. No offense taken."

"And, Charlie, thanks for coming out to check on them. Look at you! You need to get to Doc now."

...

Everyone at Doc's office was in a state of shock over Maggie and the children. While they waited for Doc to read the x-rays, they talked among themselves, Lindsay, the Kellers, Kathryn and Mildred.

Lindsay was in tears. "Oh, Lord, if anything happens to any of them, I don't know what I'll do. Who could have done such a thing? And in Serenity! Do you think Michael could be behind this?"

"I wouldn't put it past him," Caroline said. "But, on the other hand, he got what he wanted. The judge did grant him visiting rights and said she'd consider giving him more privileges if he continues to improve. I wouldn't think he'd do anything to jeopardize that. Who else could have a grudge against Maggie?"

"I had mentioned to Tom that she was concerned about our relationship and didn't understand why he never came to visit here. But he and I are back together now. And, other than thinking it was none of her business, I don't believe he held any animosity toward her. Besides, he doesn't know what she looks like or where she lives."

Caroline said, "What about those folks at the nursing home?"

Lindsay picked up on that right away. "What could they possibly have to do with Maggie?" Lindsay asked.

As soon as she'd mentioned it, Caroline regretted it. She knew Lindsay wasn't aware that Maggie and Ross had tried to check up on Tom and that the search had led them there.

CHAPTER 37

Caroline was relieved when Charlie joined in changing the focus of the conversation. "Whoever's behind this if I ever get my hands on them I'll…" Charlie had become highly agitated as Doc rejoined them carrying the x-rays. He held his hand up to quiet the room.

"We're all upset about this. This behavior isn't doing anyone any good. And you, Charlie, you've got to calm down. Your blood pressure's way up. I'm going to give you a mild sedative."

"I don't want to take anything; I'm fine," Charlie said. "I just want to find Maggie and those little ones and get them home safe."

"You've got a broken ankle, Charlie. You're going to the hospital to have it set. And between your injuries and your concern, I think a sedative is called for."

"I'll drive him," Caroline said. She had become so nervous over the events of the day and now this, that her hands trembled as she reached out for Charlie's arm.

"No, Caroline," Doc commanded. "I'm the doctor, and I'm giving the orders today. You're in no state for that. We'll call an ambulance for Charlie. I'm going to have Mildred drive you over. They might keep him overnight. Anyway, I don't want you to drive alone. I think you could use something to calm you, too."

...

Maggie's awareness was returning slowly. Her wrists were bound tightly in front of her. Her fingers were numb. She was blindfolded. She could hear the children talking behind her. They were riding. The road was smooth. She assumed they were in the burgundy Marquee he had loaded the car seats into. She must remain still. He must think she's still sleeping. She didn't want him to put that awful cloth over her face again.

His phone beeped. He pressed a button and said, "Go ahead."

She listened.

"Where are you?" A male voice asked.

"I'm almost there. I have her and the two kids. Went off without a hitch. Did you make the arrangements?"

"Yes," the voice returned. But she couldn't charter the plane until day after tomorrow."

Oh, Lord, no! He's taking us away. I only have two days!

"Are you there now?" He asked.

"Yes, we are. It's already been on the news. It'll make the headlines in the evening papers."

"See you soon. I'm almost at the turn now." He flipped the turn signal on.

Maggie felt the car slow then turn to the left. The road instantly became bumpy. It wasn't paved. It had to be dirt, as she didn't hear any gravel being spread about beneath the tires.

He switched on the car radio and searched the channels until he found a news station. The story was just wrapping up.

"Damn," he said. That was all.

It had been about the Birchwood Manor Nursing Home. Maggie had no idea what the report had been, just the mention of the name. The story wasn't repeated while the radio was on.

Maggie thought it was between ten and fifteen minutes after they turned onto the bumpy road before the car came to a stop. He got out and left the car for a moment. Then he returned.

He took the children out and left. He came back for her. She remained limp. He lifted her and carried her up two steps. He used his leg to push the door wider. He took a few strides then lowered her onto a piece of furniture. It was a sofa. She felt him untying her blindfold. He freed her hands. The children were at her side calling her name. She was finally going to get to see where he had brought them. She must play this right. And keep her wits about her!

...

When Lindsay got off work, she called Tom on his cell phone. He didn't answer, so she left a message for him asking him to return her call.

She left the clinic and stopped by the *As You Like It café* and ordered carry-out to take to Ross. She felt he wouldn't eat if someone didn't make sure he did. She could only imagine how upset he was. Maggie and those children were his life.

When Ross had called the clinic to check on Charlie, he had told Doc he was going to stay home tonight in case anyone attempted to contact him about his family. Lindsay phoned ahead to let him know she was coming.

Ross opened the door as soon as she rang the bell. His hair was disheveled and his five o'clock shadow was heavy. His eyes looked dull as if he had a bad headache.

"I brought you something to eat," she said. He followed her out to the kitchen, and she put the bag of food on the table.

"That's good of you, Lindsay. But I couldn't eat anything now."

"I understand your not being hungry, but you need something. Have you had any word from anyone?"

"Sheriff Barton called. Said there's a statewide alert out for them."

"Is there anything I can do to help with anything?"

"I've been rummaging through desk drawers to see if I could find a number for Maggie's friend, Robyn. I don't think

Michael's involved. But I still want to talk to him. He got some of what he wanted, and I don't think he'd risk losing that. But, we never did get an address or phone number for him. It was left that he'd contact us, and he never did which I find strange. Anyway, I thought Robyn may know how to reach him. I called information for her number and it's unlisted."

"I wouldn't know where Maggie keeps things like that."

Ross nodded. "Me either." They talked a little more. Ross finally agreed to eat some of the carry-out if Lindsay would join him.

A short while after they finished, the phone rang. Ross dashed for it. There was no answer on the other end of the line. "Hello, hello," he shouted into the receiver. He immediately heard the disconnect tone. He pressed the caller ID button, it showed unavailable. Dejectedly, he returned to the table.

"If there's nothing else I can do here tonight, I'll head back to town and check on Caroline and Charlie," Lindsay said. "If they kept Charlie in overnight, and she came back, I'll offer to spend the night with her. She was terribly upset today."

"I think that's a good idea, Lindsay. She was doing so well these past few years and now all of this; she doesn't need to be alone tonight."

Lindsay rose and started for the front door. Ross followed her. "Thanks," he said. "You're a true friend." He reached for the knob and opened the door for her.

She turned back to him. "You said you've looked in all the desk drawers for Robyn's number. Did you look in Maggie's dresser drawers?"

"No. Why would she keep it in there?"

"It's a woman thing. We keep things in our dresser drawers, especially things from the past."

"It's worth a try. Come on back. Since it was your idea, let's see if we can find anything there."

Lindsay followed him up the stairs and into his and Maggie's bedroom. Ross pulled her top dresser drawer out and searched hastily through it while Lindsay sat on the foot of the bed and waited. "Nothing here," he said closing the drawer. He repeated the same procedure with the other drawers then turned back to her, looking disappointed. "No luck, but thanks anyway."

"Let me take a look in the top drawer," Lindsay said. "That's where I keep things like that."

"Be my guest," he said.

Lindsay rose from the bed and went over to the drawer Ross had pulled out for her. She ran her hands down both sides and across the front underneath the clothing. Then she reached way to the back of the drawer and her hand struck a packet of papers. She removed them and handed them to Ross and went back to sit down.

Ross stood and began sorting through them. He quickly found a small address book. As he opened it, papers dropped to the floor. He continued focusing on the booklet. "Here it is; here's Robyn's number. I'll call her now.

Lindsay got up and went to pick up the several items that Ross had dropped. They were photos. She looked at them one by one. "Look Ross, is Robyn in this picture? He turned back to look and took the picture from her.

"Yes, that's Robyn right there and of course, you recognize Maggie, and that's…."

"Oh my God, Ross!" She shrieked.

He stopped mid-sentence and turned to Lindsay. Her face was ghastly white. Her left arm was wrapped about her stomach. "Are you okay?" He asked

CHAPTER 38

Lindsay tried to speak but no words came.

Ross stepped closer and reached out to steady her. "What is it? Are you hurting somewhere?"

Without speaking, she handed him the photo she had been looking at.

He took it from her. "That's Michael. I didn't realize she still had a picture of him."

Lindsay shook her head vigorously. "No, Ross. That's my Tom! Oh my God! That's my Tom. Now I understand!" She began to sob. "This is all my fault! Maggie and the children are gone…I can't reach Tom…I'd be willing to bet he has them!"

"That's incredible!" Ross stared at the picture of Michael and Maggie for a few seconds without speaking as he turned it all over in his mind. Then he shifted his attention back to Lindsay.

"No, it isn't your fault," he said. "But I bet you're right, and thank you, Lindsay!"

"Yes, it is my fault! He pumped me for information about my friends. And, I, like a big dumb fool, fed it to him."

"Look, you helped me find this picture. Thank God Maggie kept it, and thank you for being here with me when we looked through her drawer. If you hadn't been here, I'd have shoved the picture back into the drawer, called Robyn and we still wouldn't know who we were looking for."

"Then you aren't angry with me?" She asked.

He grabbed her and hugged her. "No, you've given us what we need to narrow the search down. Thank you, Lindsay."

Lindsay looked crushed.

Ross became keenly aware of the fact that the news had been a God- send to him but very devastating to Lindsay's love life. "Lindsay, I'm sorry. This has to be rough on you."

She looked at him and gave him a faint smile. "Don't worry about me, I'll be fine. Now, what are you waiting for? Go call Sheriff Barton! We have to get your family back!" Her smile brightened a bit.

As soon as she left, Ross put in a call to the Sheriff. He didn't reach him but left a message for him to return his call. He didn't hear from him all night.

...

Ross slept poorly but morning found him a bit more hopeful. They finally had something he considered concrete to go on in the search for his family. Robyn had been unable to help him. She had confided to him that Maggie had called her months earlier to ask for information about Michael also. After Ross hung up, he had to admit to himself that Maggie hadn't been paranoid after all. She had been right to worry about Michael. And perhaps she actually had seen him at the hospital when Tyler was a patient there.

He put in another call to the sheriff. Barton was expected in momentarily. He'd been working on a case all night. Ross made a pot of coffee and went outside to get the morning paper and wait for the sheriff's call. He hoped the case was his and it had been fruitful, but he doubted it had. He'd have heard something by now if there'd been any significant breaks.

He opened the paper and read the headline staring at him.

OWNERS OF BIRCHWOOD MANNOR NURSING HOME DISAPPEAR

Not just a coincidence, Ross thought. *I'd bet a million dollars this is all tied together.* He devoured the article as he sipped his coffee. The first two bodies exhumed had shown large traces of a drug which was not named. Exhuming of the remaining bodies was being expedited. The authorities had gone to the nursing home to question the administrator and learned that neither he nor his wife, the personnel director, had shown up that day. A spokesman for the facility said that wasn't unusual. When the authorities went to their private residence there was no one there. A neighbor woman spoke anonymously. She told the police she had seen the couple load suitcases into their SUV and drive away late the day before. There was now an APB out on them and their SUV. The phone rang before he finished the rest of the article.

Ross picked up. It was Sheriff Dominic Barton. "Have you read the morning paper?"

"I have. Hell of a mess." The sheriff replied.

"Maggie's disappearance and the Birchwood Manor incidents are connected. I'm sure of it! I have something to tell you, and it's a long story. Can we do it by phone? I'm still sticking close to home in case Maggie finds a way to contact me. Her purse was shoved under the seat on the passenger side. Her cell phone wasn't in it. I'm praying that she has it…that she'll find a way to use it."

"I agree. You need to stay at home today. Fire away. I'm gonna record our conversation if you don't mind." Barton's deep voice boomed.

"Good idea," Ross said. "He began the tale with Maggie and Lindsay's first trip to Bromley, then his and Maggie's first visit and ended with them going to Birchwood Manor.

Twenty five minutes later when Ross finished, Barton said. "That's great. I think you're on to something. We'll get started exploring that avenue right away."

"Sounds good."

Dixie Land

"By the way, Ross. The press will probably be showing up at your place any time now. I've already talked to them. I've told them we're looking for any information we can get...that we have no clues at the present time. We all need to stick to that story. Don't want any information released to help the abductor."

"I agree. I'm going to call Lindsay and tell her to keep what we learned last night to herself. I should have told her that last night. I hope I'm not too late!"

As he lifted the receiver, he glanced at his watch. She should still be at home. He started to dial and realized he didn't know her number. He cursed under his breath as he went to caller ID and looked back to the previous night's call from her.

He quickly dialed her number. It rang three times before she answered. He put her on speaker and reached for a pad and pen to write down her number for future reference.

"I hope you haven't told anyone about discovering Tom's identity last night!"

"I...oh, Ross, I did..."

"Who?" Ross demanded.

"Only Caroline and Charlie. I was so upset when I got home. I needed to talk to someone."

"No one else? You didn't try to call Tom...Michael again, did you?"

"Ross, I was upset, not stupid. Of course not! And I didn't hear from him."

"I gotta, go. Don't tell another soul. I'll call Charlie and ask them to keep our secret." He hung up and dialed again.

Caroline answered.

She barely got "hello," out of her mouth when Ross said, "You haven't told anyone about Tom, have you?" He held his breath as he waited for her answer.

CHAPTER 39

"Of course not," Caroline said. "I just asked Charlie to go out and catch Lindsay before she leaves and tell her not to be talking about it either. I think this is a breakthrough, and you know how word travels in this little town. We don't need to put any information out that would help that awful man."

"I just got off the phone with her, and she promised not to tell anyone else. Charlie telling her the same will just re-emphasize it. Thanks, Caroline."

...

Captives

Maggie opened her eyes slowly and looked around the room. Her hands still tingled from their restraints. She rubbed them together to stimulate the circulation, then she opened her arms to her children. They nestled against her on the sofa. Michael stood over them watching.

"You're finally waking. Welcome to your temporary new home."

Maggie continued to hold her children close and assure them that everything would be okay. Momentarily, she rose to a sitting position and shifted around to rest her feet on the floor, still holding a child in each arm. She looked about the crude cabin. It was small, cramped and musty smelling. To the right she saw a closed door, maybe a bedroom or perhaps a bathroom. Behind her was a small open kitchen. She heard the sound of what might be a generator running. It must be their power source. She hoped it would take the damp chill out of the place. In one corner of the room sat several suitcases. Next to them were see-through plastic bags of canned goods. Looking through the dirty, bare front window, she saw nothing but open space outside.

Michael watched her take in the surroundings. "Don't worry; your next destination will be much more spacious, quite lovely in fact."

"What do you mean next destination? Where are you taking us?"

"In due time, not for you to worry about now." He began to pace the floor. "I have money now, Maggie, lots of it. We can start building a life together just as we were always meant to."

Maggie watched him as he walked about the room. She thought his eyes looked wild, as if he was on something, but she dare not let him know she suspected it. *Be cool, Maggie, be cool. There are more lives here than yours to be concerned about. Gain his confidence; don't make an enemy of him.*

"You're even more beautiful now that you've had a child, our child. I've never met a woman to compare with you. I should never have let you leave me. And you're different. Those others, they were so easy, especially Lindsay. And then I could hardly get rid of them. But you, you left me...not like those clinging..."

"Then **you** are Tom. I wondered why he never came around."

"Yes. Wasn't that clever? I staged it all. It was the perfect way to keep track of you...to learn everything about you...everything that was happening in your life. I knew right away when you got that little girl from Melanie."

Maggie was so glad she hadn't told Lindsay who Keri's real father was.

Michael was still ranting, "And Lindsay was so gullible, so loose tongued. I even knew when you and she came looking for me...." His voice droned on. He was pacing and rambling.

Maggie let him continue while her mind shifted to thoughts of escaping. She was trying to devise a plan. But absolutely nothing was coming to her.

...

Later, Michael opened a can of pork and beans and some Vienna sausages for their evening meal, promising her grand meals in the new home he would take them to. He was kind enough to her and to the children. He had even brought some toys for them to play with. Though they were still very quiet, Tyler and Keri seemed to feel safer now that Maggie was awake and Michael allowed them stay close to her.

When they finished eating, he showed her the bags of clothing he had for both children and some for her also. He had even bought pull-up pants for Tyler. Maggie said as little as possible all evening. The last thing on earth she wanted to do was antagonize Michael. His behavior seemed so erratic to her that she was constantly on edge and desperately trying not to show it.

When bedtime came, he said, "You take them into the bedroom there," he pointed toward the door on the right, "and put them to bed. Everything you need for them is in this bag." He lifted a plastic bag and handed it to her. "Then you come out here with me."

She rose and went into the bedroom with the children. It was dark. She found a table light and turned it on. The only window in the room was boarded up. There was a crude bathroom on one side of the room with no door. There were linens on the bed and toilet paper in the bathroom, even a jug of water sitting on the floor. Obviously, he had been planning this for sometime and had come previously to prepare for their arrival. That must be why they hadn't heard from him about visiting Tyler. He was working on their abduction.

She dressed Tyler and Keri for bed and stayed with them, singing softly, until they fell asleep. At one point, Michael opened the door and peered in to check on them.

When she returned to the front room he seemed to have mellowed. He no longer paced as he had earlier. *He must be coming down off whatever he was on,* she thought.

He took her hand in his and pulled her to the sofa and sat down. He tried to kiss her. His breath had a strange odor, like nothing she had ever smelled before.

"Please, Michael, not tonight," she implored. "Today has been so unsettling, and I'm exhausted."

He pulled back. "I can understand that." He grew quiet.

They sat quietly on the sofa for what seemed an interminable amount of time to Maggie. When she could stand it no longer, she said. "Michael, I'm so tired, and I don't feel well. Please let me go into the bedroom and sleep with my children tonight."

He looked at her rather poignantly. "You're a wonderful mother, Maggie. Okay, go."

She left him, went into the bedroom and closed the door behind her. She was relieved to see her children still sleeping. She heard Michael push a piece of furniture against the door, and a sound as he'd flopped down on it.

As she slipped out of the light-weight jacket she'd worn all day, she heard a little bump as it hit the only wooden chair in the room. She reached into the right pocket and felt her cell phone. Her heart quickened. She removed it and switched it on. It still held half a charge. She wouldn't chance making a call tonight. She quickly turned it off. Perhaps she'd have a better opportunity tomorrow to contact Ross.

CHAPTER 40

Serenity

Shortly after Ross hung up with the sheriff, his doorbell rang. He hurried to answer it. "Oh, Lil! Come in."

She embraced him then stood back at arms length. "Ross, I had to come see how you were doing. Betty's covering for me. Look at you, you're a sight. Have you had anything to eat since all this happened?"

"Yes, I have. Lindsay brought dinner last night."

"Any word at all yet?"

He shook his head. "Nothing."

His phone rang. He hurried to answer it. "Hello," he said loudly. "Oh, hello." He covered the speaker with his hand and told Lil it was Melanie's lawyer. He returned to the caller and listened. Midway through the conversation, he heard a beep. He looked at the caller ID. It was Maggie's cell number. "Gotta hang up." He pressed flash, put the phone on speaker, grabbed paper and pen to make notes and shoved a paper at Lil. She stepped to his side. She found a pen and began to take notes also.

There was a great deal of static on the line. Maggie's voice crackled and faded in and out. They could hear only snatches of her conversation.

"Ross,…okay… now. Don't talk…ju… listen… Michael … us, …outside …. owners …. Nursing…home. … battery dying…"

"Can you speak up," Ross shouted. "I can hardly hear you."

Maggie continued. "Can't, Michael …hear…don't know…long... h…in wilderness …" static interrupted them again… "early … morning" more static. "heard …. sounded … gunshots… crude …cabins … generators … propane tanks…dirt road leading in… overheard … talking…charter plane… some … tomorrow…Drove … hour …. here. Michael… crazy… Tom. hope…

Ross and Lil heard a male voice shout in the distance.

"What in hell are you doing?" It had to be Michael.

The sound of a scuffle came over the speaker phone, and the phone went dead.

"I've got to get hold of Barton!" Ross was frantic.

...

Captives

"I trusted you! Give me that damn phone!" he jerked it from Maggie's trembling hand. His face was scarlet as he raged at her.

"It's dead," she cried. "I couldn't reach anyone." She burst into tears.

He put the phone to his ear and listened. "Okay," he said. "But you shouldn't have even tried." He reached the door in two strides and stepped outside. Maggie saw him heave her phone with all his strength. It landed a great distance from the cabin in some tall weeds.

Oh dear God, she prayed, please let Ross have heard enough to help them find us. As she sat on the couch sobbing, Tyler and Keri ran to her and put their arms around her. Tyler was in tears. Michael stepped over to them and tried to comfort Maggie and the boy.

"You go away. You're bad," Keri said defiantly.

Michael glared at the child.

Maggie glared back at Michael and held her hand up to shield Keri. "It's alright, dear," she said to the little girl. "I'm okay." Maggie blotted Keri's eyes with the back of her hand.

Michael stepped away from them and went into the bedroom.

"Keri, don't say anything to make him mad," Maggie whispered in her ear. "I'm fine. We're all going to be okay."

...

Serenity

While Ross spoke to the sheriff, Lil had an idea of her own. She took out her cell phone and dialed her nephew Kevin's number. He had known Michael very well at one time. Perhaps he could shed some light on this location. At least it was worth a try. His secretary said he was in conference.

"I'm his aunt, Lillian Bingham," she told the woman. "This is a matter of life and death. I must talk to him immediately!"

Lil's tone did the trick. She was transferred to Kevin.

As soon as Ross finished talking with Sheriff Barton, Lil told him she had called Kevin to see if he had any ideas as to where Michael could possibly have taken them. Kevin planned to come to Serenity as soon as he could get away from the office today. He mentioned a place Michael spoke of going to as a boy. It was in North Carolina, he went with his father to hunt and fish.

Ross and Lil left the house. Ross drove to the sheriff's office. Lil headed for home to wait for her nephew.

...

Sheriff Barton had a map of the state spread out on his desk going over it with a magnifying glass. "I'm gonna have to make an appointment with the optometrist" he said. "I'm having trouble reading some of this."

Ross had both his and Lil's notes with him. He handed them to Barton. "We' don't have much time," Ross said. He joined the sheriff over the map.

Dixie Land

"We've had about twenty calls from all over the state today," Barton said. "Most of them are wild goose chases according to what you were able to make out from Maggie's phone call. I'm focusing on the eastern part of the state. They could be on the outskirts of the Fort Bragg area; she could have heard gun fire from a rifle range."

"From what I could make out of what she said, she thought it was about an hour away from here." Ross said.

"Actually," Barton said. "I have my doubts about the Fort. Bragg area. In the last few years security has really tightened around the base. I think the whole surrounding area is well patrolled."

"You're probably right about that. My guess is that they could be somewhere in the vicinity of a hunting reserve. There are several in the eastern part of the state. And it has to be a place with enough area for a plane to land and take off, from what I could make out of what Maggie was trying to tell me. Lil called her nephew. You know he and Michael were pretty thick a few years back. It almost got Kevin in a lot of trouble with the law board. Anyway, he's on his way here. He told Lil he had a vague idea of where they might hole up. He'll be here this afternoon. Lil's going to bring him over as soon as he arrives."

Barton's phone rang. He picked up. "Yes," he said. "Thanks for returning my call." He turned to Ross and mouthed, SBI.

Ross continued looking at the map, concentrating on the entire area surrounding Serenity an hour out in every direction.

...

"Very interesting," Barton said when he got off the phone with the State Bureau of Investigation. "They, too, are convinced this has a direct connection to the nursing home deaths. This isn't for publication yet, but, they have the results in from the first four autopsies."

Ross looked up from the map. "What did they show?"

"Each of the bodies contained un-naturally large amounts of potassium chloride."

"That makes perfect sense," Ross said. "Potassium Chloride is the drug used on criminals who are executed by lethal injection. It stops the heart pretty quickly. With the elderly in a nursing home, it's natural to assume they died of a heart attack. They've really tightened up on dispensing the drug in recent years, but I guess a doctor could still get his hands on it without too much of a problem. They probably ordered it in small quantities and built up a store of it to use periodically."

"Like in an acceptable time frame after the new wills were signed," Barton said.

"Exactly. And that would explain Michael's, a.k.a Tom's, periodic visits to the area. They probably had him call on the nursing home whenever they were ready to 'dispose' of another resident. That would explain why Lindsay only saw him once in a while."

The phone rang again, Barton picked up. "Oh, Lil, thanks for letting us know. We'll look for you in the next thirty minutes." He hung up. "The nephew's almost to Serenity and then they'll be right over. Two SBI agents should arrive between 2:00 and 3:00 p.m."

Ross felt his adrenalin beginning to kick in.

...

Captives
Afternoon

Michael had been pacing for the last thirty minutes. There was a knock at the door. It seemed to unnerve him. He turned quickly and looked out the window, then hurried to open the door. The couple from the nursing home entered. The man handed Michael a small packet of something and he went into the bedroom with it.

"Well, we meet again," Evelyn Anderson said to Maggie.

Maggie just looked at her.

Keri said, "Who are you?"

"I'm Mrs. Anderson, and this is my husband, Daniel," she said frostily. "And I firmly believe that children should be seen and not heard from, little girl."

Maggie reached out to Keri and pulled her close.

Michael returned momentarily appearing much calmer than when he went into the bedroom.

He and the newcomers stepped into the kitchen and spoke in hushed tones.

Maggie and the children remained on the sofa. She whispered to them to stay very quiet. She strained to hear what the three were discussing. She was sure it had something to do with the plan to leave the area tomorrow. Try as she might to hear, she only caught a word here and there. It wasn't much help. She could only pray that there would be enough time for Ross to find them.

By the end of the day, Maggie's nerves were frayed and she was finding it difficult to hide her despair. Still she must, and she also must find a way to stall their departure tomorrow, but how?

After dark, she told Michael she was putting the children to bed and that she was going to turn in with them. "I have an upset stomach," she said. "The smell of that tuna you opened tonight made me feel very queasy."

"After tomorrow we'll have better meals. And in our new home, Tyler will have his own room and you and I will have ours."

A terrible chill shot through her as she stepped into the bedroom. She heard him push the sofa against the door as he had the night before. As she lay down on the bed with Tyler and Keri, Michael's last words played repeatedly in her mind. What did they mean? Was it a just slip of the tongue or did he plan to leave Keri behind, or did he have something even worse in mind for her? *Oh, dear God,* she prayed silently. *Please help us escape, please let me keep both of my children safe. Let Ross find us, Please!* Silent tears rolled down her cheeks. She rested her hands on her abdomen. *And if I am pregnant,* and she was beginning to be quite sure she was, *don't let any harm come to this new little life.*

...

Serenity

The SBI agents were already there when Lil and Kevin walked into the sheriff's office thirty minutes after Lil's call.

Lil collapsed her umbrella and shook it off. "Whew! What a downpour! But I guess we need it."

After introductions were made, Barton passed the map to Kevin. "Any of these locations ring a bell with you about the place he told you about?" He had drawn a circle with Serenity at the center of all of the areas within an hour's driving distance.

Kevin studied the map for a few seconds. "Seems to me it wasn't very far from Ft. Bragg. Maybe in the Rockingham area. I was actually there once, but we arrived after dark and I wasn't driving and it was dark when we left also."

As the group made plans, Barton's assistant was in the outer office speaking with the authorities in the Fayetteville area checking out the possibility of an area near the post where the abductors could be holding Maggie and the children.

When she got off the phone she joined the others. "Excuse me," she began. The room quieted. "They feel it's highly unlikely. The areas close enough to the firing range to hear shots are heavily patrolled. There aren't any hunting reserves near there either."

"Let's concentrate on the Rockingham area," SBI Agent Bob Hendrix said. "I'll call ahead and get the authorities there on it and we'll head that way about 5:00 a.m. It's senseless to leave in the dark with all this rain to contend with when we aren't sure where we're going."

Ross had been pacing. "I'm not waiting! I'm heading to the area tonight. If I can't do anything tonight, at least I'll get an earlier start in the morning."

Barton had a stern expression. "I know how upset you have to be. But, don't you go off and do something half-cocked and cause more problems for us. We'll be there early. You wait for us."

Kevin addressed the sheriff. "I'm going with him," he said. "I may recognize the area when we get closer to it. And I have a history with Michael. I got him out of a pretty tough spot a few years back. I may be able to reason with him about this too. We'll see you first thing tomorrow."

Lil looked relieved. "I'll call Caroline and Charlie and let them know what's developing. They're worried sick over this. Charlie's still learning how to use his crutches, or I'm sure he'd be right here with us."

Ross and Kevin headed out of town in Ross's car.

Captives

The skies had opened up at dusk and continued to pour down on the area all night. Maggie slept fitfully. At 6:00 a.m. she heard Michael cursing. He was talking on the phone. From his end of the conversation, she knew it was Daniel Anderson.

"Damn! Of all times for it to rain like hell! What's the forecast for today?" He was quiet for a moment. "Damn!" he said again. "Call him back and tell him to try to make it in this afternoon. We could even go out and try to burn off some of the moisture." Michael said.

She heard him walk away from the bedroom door. The sound of the front door opening and closing ended her ability to eavesdrop.

Thank you, Lord, she prayed silently. *Please keep the rain coming.* Maggie had always been a firm believer that if you asked for something and received it, it was important to give thanks.

This would help her and her children. Perhaps give them even another day, if the rain would only continue. She prayed for anything that would give them more time for help to find them.

...

The weather began to clear mid-morning, the clouds dissipated and the sun shown brightly.

Chapter 41

Ross and Kevin

The rain had been so heavy that it had taken the men two hours to reach Rockingham. They found a motel and got two rooms. They would have to continue the search in the daylight.

Ross barely slept. He prayed repeatedly for a break in the weather and guidance in finding his family.

He met Kevin in the lobby the next morning at the appointed hour. It was still raining but had slowed considerably from the prior evening. They left as dawn was breaking and rode to the outskirts of town. They explored several rural roads and found nothing familiar to Kevin.

"I think we need to go back to town and ask some directions. Let's start with the police department," Ross said. "This is a waste of time."

They stopped at a gas station and got directions to the law enforcement offices. The policeman on duty was already familiar with the case having heard from Sheriff Barton's office the previous afternoon.

"You're in the wrong location," he said. "I told them yesterday, there's no hunting reserve here, it's over beyond Laurinburg."

"I'd have sworn it was here," Kevin said. "I'm sorry about that, Ross. As I said, it was years ago, and it was dark when we came and left."

As they headed toward Laurinburg, Ross looked at his cell phone. It was turned off. "I wonder how long it's been off," he mumbled. "He dialed the sheriff's number."

"Yes, I know, I just discovered it. Anything new?" When their conversation ended, he relayed the news to Kevin. "He knew we went to the wrong location, but couldn't reach us and Lil didn't know your number."

"It wouldn't have done any good. I left my phone in my car yesterday when we got to the sheriff's office," Kevin said.

"Barton and the SBI agents should be in Laurinburg when we arrive. This just occurred to me," Ross said. "Maggie mentioned something about a generator. They can't run without fuel, and in the boondocks, that means they'd need a propane tank. As soon as we get to town, let's see if we can find if there have been any deliveries to any remote areas in the last few weeks."

Ross called Barton again and asked him to start checking with the gas company to save time.

...

Captives

Michael had been uptight all morning. He was short with the children and with Maggie. She suspected he was on something again. He and the Andersons exchanged several calls. From what she could make out from the snippets of conversation she heard, the plane would arrive in the afternoon and try to land.

When Michael went into the bedroom and shut the door, she hurried to the window to assess the ground. It looked very soggy with puddles of water standing in the lower spots. She doubted a plane could land safely let alone take off again. She hoped they would have another day. She returned to the sofa.

Tyler and Keri had climbed down when Michael left them. They were playing with some of the toys he had given them. The bedroom door opened and Michael stepped out. The little ones dropped their toys and scampered onto Maggie's lap.

"Why are you afraid of me," Michael asked sounding much kinder than he had earlier.

Neither child answered, just snuggled against Maggie.

"I'm sorry I was cross earlier," he continued. "How would you like to stand at the window and watch me build a fire?"

"Fire?" Tyler said.

"Yes," Michael replied. "We have to dry up the ground so the airplane can come and take us for a ride."

Maggie's heart sank.

...

Search Party

It took the gas company only a few minutes to access the last month's records, it took them nearly thirty minutes to contact the driver who serviced that part of the county. Ross paced as they waited for the return call. The company was actually located between Laurinburg and a neighboring town.

While Barton was making calls, SBI Agent Wilcox made and received a number of calls also. When he concluded, he was very satisfied with the results of what he had found. With the exception of Barton, he kept it to himself to insure its success.

As Ross waited for the information to be gathered, time seemed to stand still. He found the delay of waiting for a call back from the driver on the route agonizing. Nearly an hour from the time the search began, Sheriff Barton's phone rang.

"Yes. Yes thanks." As he listened, Barton shook his head. He motioned for paper and pen, and began making notes. Then he scratched some of them out. He asked a few questions, and listened again. He finally said, "That makes good sense, but hurry. We're running out of time!"

Chapter 42

Captives

They hadn't gone to the window. But when Maggie heard loud voices outside, she stepped over to look out. Keri followed her. Michael and Daniel appeared to be arguing. As their voices grew louder, Tyler ran up and bumped against the window frame.

Daniel, who faced the direction of the cabin, shifted his attention from Michael to the window. Michael turned also. Seeing they were being watched, the arguing ceased. Daniel nodded his head as he removed a cell phone from his pocket and appeared to make a call. He didn't talk long.

Then Michael removed a large box of matches from his car, held the car keys up so Maggie could see that he still had them in his possession, and the two men headed off toward the distant field.

The children returned to their toys. Maggie continued to watch. If only she could go out and locate her cell phone. But that would be futile, surely the battery would be completely gone by now as low as it was when she was trying to contact Ross. And the long, heavy rain had probably damaged it. It would be useless to her.

After a few minutes of walking the field, Michael and Daniel started back toward the cabins. When Michael entered the cabin, he looked pleased.

"It isn't as bad out there as we thought it would be. The plane will be able to land after all. Let's start getting the things we're going to take with us together."

...

The Search Party

The driver from the propane company arrived half-an-hour after he and the sheriff finished talking. He pulled up to the local police station where the search party was waiting in vehicles ready to roll.

He called out of his open window, "Follow me." He swung his delivery truck around to a forty-five degree angle and headed away from town with a caravan of two police cars and Ross's vehicle in close pursuit.

"Damn! I hope we aren't too late," Ross said. "Everything that could hold us up seems to have." His head was splitting. He reached up and kneaded the back of his neck.

"Why don't you pull over and let me drive?" Kevin asked.

"I'm fine." Ross said in a steely voice.

Kevin knew it was senseless to argue with him. He'd feel the same if it was Carley they needed to rescue.

...

Captives

Maggie had done everything in her power not to become confrontational with Michael. She wanted nothing to upset him to the point that he would hurt the children or her. She didn't want that awful cloth over her face again. She didn't want him to force himself on her either. She had prayed silently and unceasingly that Ross would find her...that he had been able to make enough sense out of her garbled message to give the authorities enough clues to find them. Now her hopes grew dimmer by the minute. She must do something to stall their departure.

"How soon are you expecting the plane?" She asked, working at keeping her voice calm. "And where is it taking us?"

Michael glanced at his watch. "It should be here within the next hour. Out of the country. Are you eager to leave?

He has to be on something to ask me that, Maggie thought. But she said, "No, Michael. I think this is a mistake. You don't really love me. The judge gave you visiting rights. You said that was what you wanted. Please, just take us home. We won't press any charges, I promise you. You can visit us. You can see Tyler whenever you want to. We'll just forget this ever happened if you take us back now."

He threw his head back and laughed. "I can't do that. Do you think I'm stupid, Maggie? I don't buy that for a minute. As soon as you were home safe, the police would have an all points bulletin out on me. And, yes, you would press charges."

"No! I swear to you. I wouldn't."

"Ross would. That's a certainty. And besides, some other people are looking for me, too."

Maggie didn't pursue that last comment at this time. She stayed on track, "No, he wouldn't...not if I asked him not to." Maggie glanced at her children. Tyler was oblivious to their conversation, but she wasn't so sure Keri was. She thought the child understood at least some of what was being said.

"Oh yes he would!" Michael said. "I certainly would if I were in his shoes. But I have you now, and you and Tyler are going with me."

"Why do you say Tyler and me?"

CHAPTER 43

"Because that's who I'm taking. He's mine. And you and I will have more children…more boys," he said.

"You can't leave Keri behind." Maggie was well aware that Keri was now listening to every word they were saying. Keri rose from the floor and went to Maggie. She wrapped her arms around Maggie's neck and began to cry. Tears rolled down Maggie's cheeks and intermingled with Keri's.

"No, Michael. None of us wants to go with you. But you have a choice. You take all of us or none."

"You forget who's in control here. I don't have a choice. You do. You and Tyler can go with me, or you can all die."

Someone banged on the door.

Oh, dear God, please let it be help. Maggie's heart raced.

Michael glanced at his watch, hurried to the door and pulled it open. "Right on time," he said to Daniel and Eve. The men had been referring to Evelyn Anderson as Eve since they arrived here. And Maggie thought of her as Eve, the temptress in the Bible.

Daniel spoke, "Let's get your luggage loaded and we'll take it out to the field. We'll be back for you." Michael helped them pack their SUV then returned to Maggie.

Keri was still hanging onto Maggie for dear life. She was crying even harder now. Tyler began to cry, too.

Trying to focus his attention away from the children, Maggie asked, "Michael, how did you get hooked up with those two?"

"We go way back. We're business partners and very successful. I told you, I'm quite wealthy now. Our lives are going to be good."

"Partners? How?"

"We manage a charitable foundation. I'm a specialist in geriatric care now."

Since when? Maggie wondered.

Michael continued. "They called me periodically when they needed a particular treatment on one of their residents."

"*Oh, my Lord, Michael **was** killing those dear sweet people for them!*" Maggie was even more terrified with this confession. Perhaps she had suspected it subconsciously when she learned they were together. She had tried not to think about it. But to hear the words coming from his lips now…it put her into even more of a panic. He was ruthless…heartless… an unscrupulous sociopath! He had killed before. She now believed, without a doubt, that he wouldn't hesitate to kill again.

She gazed out of the window and saw the Andersons driving toward their cabin. She began to tremble. What would the next moments hold for them all?

...

The Rescuers

The caravan of rescuers turned onto the gravel road that led to the isolated cabins near the hunting reserve. Even with the bright sun, the ground was still wet and extremely rutty. The lead vehicle slowed to a crawl. Ross felt his agitation grow. They were almost there…they mustn't be too late. Impatience swept through him, he felt a vise-like pain in his chest.

...

Captives

The four adults and two children waited in the open field as the plane neared the landing area. As it came closer, Maggie

Dixie Land

could make out that it was a Beechcraft with N90CT written on the side. Maggie had been in one of those several years ago. She knew that they held seven passengers plus the pilot. There would be plenty of room for Keri. Michael had let her bring Keri this far, and Maggie didn't intend to let go of her. As the plane touched down onto the ground and taxied toward its passengers, the convoy of rescuers drove into the opening near the three cabins and sped toward the open field.

Maggie had Tyler in her arms and Keri was clinging to her waist. As she caught sight of them, relief washed over her. Hope returned. Still she knew they were a long way from safe.

The plane stopped about a hundred yards from the passengers. Barton's squad car stopped a short distance from the abductors. He jumped out of the car, pistol drawn.

Michael was wielding a gun by now, too. He had been behind Maggie when the law arrived. He grabbed Keri and jerked her roughly from Maggie's grip. He lifted the gun to her head. "Stay back. We're going to get on that plane and leave. If you don't drop your guns right now, the girl dies!" Michael shouted over the roar of the engine.

"Daddy!" Tyler shouted when Ross stepped to the front of the officers.

"Shut up, Tyler. He's not your daddy..."

"Daddy, Daddy," Tyler sobbed, arms reaching toward Ross.

Kevin stepped to Ross's side. "Michael! Stop and think about what you're doing. I can help you if you stop this now."

The Andersons were inching backward toward the plane. Barton and one other officer still had their guns drawn.

"I mean it," Michael said. "Drop the guns or she's dead. You've got to three. One..."

The rescuers froze. First Barton, then the Deputy, lowered their guns slowly onto the grass as Michael watched their every move.

Return to Serenity

    Then a single blast rang out over the noise of the aircraft engine while the rescue team watched in complete shock.

CHAPTER 44

Keri let out a blood curdling scream. Michael slumped to the ground.

The officers snatched their weapons from the ground aiming them at the Andersons and ran toward them.

Maggie swooped Keri up with her free arm and held her tightly. Keri buried her head against Maggie's neck still crying hysterically.

Ross raced to them. He wrapped his arms around them all. Maggie was shaking and crying as she fell against her husband. "Thank God, you found us in time. I love you, I love you," she repeated. "Oh thank you, Lord!"

Ross covered them with kisses. He lifted both children from his wife's arms. "Thank God, is right. I don't know what I'd have done if we hadn't," he added. They turned back to see the Andersons being cuffed and led toward the sheriff's vehicle.

Maggie distanced herself and the children from the scene. They had seen far too much already.

Ross turned toward SBI Agent Wilcox who was bending over Michael, checking for a pulse. There was none, no respirations, no signs of life. The agent examined his head. The bullet had entered the base of Michael's skull shattering the back of his head. The damage to his cerebellum at the top of the brain stem killed him instantly.

Wilcox rose, looked toward the airplane and waved. "Great shot, Josh!"

By now, the pilot had killed the plane's engine so the field was relatively quiet. "Folks, I'd like to introduce sharp-shooter, Agent Josh Barnes. Fortunately we were able to locate the company the plane had been chartered through. Their plan was to go to Canada. We replaced their pilot with one of our own. Sheriff Barton was the only person I informed ahead of time. I figured the fewer who knew, the greater the element of surprise. And that was important."

Ross shouted a thank you and Kevin gave Agent Barnes a two-thumbs-up. Ross thanked everyone there for their part in the rescue.

He turned to Kevin. "I appreciate you more than you know. We got off to a rough start, but I'm proud to call you friend now."

"Thanks." The men shook hands. Kevin went to Maggie and gave her a hug. He appeared quite emotional as he walked to the Sheriff's car to return to Serenity.

"Let's get the children away from all this," Ross said. They all headed for their car.

Maggie was exhausted but happy as Ross strapped both children into their seats. He opened her door for her. "Let me do that for you too," he said to Maggie. He kissed her as he strapped her in just as he had Tyler and Keri. "Oh, and by the way, I had a call from Melanie's lawyer," he said very quietly. "Keri is officially our little girl now. After everyone recovers from this ordeal, we'll have a celebration and tell her."

"Thank God," she whispered. "You know, I thought about telling Michael he was her father when he was threatening to leave her behind or worse yet, to kill her. I'm so glad I didn't. I'm afraid she might have understood what I said. She's been through far too much to hear something like that on top of everything else."

Ross got in the car, started it and the four Harringtons headed for Serenity. They hadn't driven long when a hush fell over the back seat. Maggie turned back to see both Tyler and Keri sleeping in their car seats.

"Bless their hearts," she said. "They're completely exhausted." She turned back and settled into her seat again. "I'd better call Caroline and Charlie and let them know we're safe. Michael threw my phone away. I'll have to use yours."

Ross handed it to her. She dialed, Caroline answered on the second ring. "Caroline, it's Maggie. We're all safe, we're with Ross and we're on our way home." She told her only a little of the rescue.

Caroline had offered to call Lil but Maggie wanted to. She didn't want Lil to feel slighted. However, she did ask Caroline to call Doc and Kathryn. When she reached Lil, Lil told her she had just hung up with Kevin. Maggie could hear the relief in Lil's voice. Then Maggie called Lindsay but got no answer. She did leave a message.

Ross said, "Lindsay was instrumental in helping us find you. She brought dinner in the night you disappeared. She helped me look for Robyn's number; I thought Robyn might have some idea of how to contact Michael. A picture of you and Michael dropped out of the address book. Lindsay was speechless when she learned that Tom and Michael were one and the same. She took it hard, I felt so bad for her."

"I'm so sorry for her too. She's going to need a lot of support," Maggie said softly.

"She is," Ross agreed.

Maggie glanced back to see that the children were still sleeping. She took a deep breath, then said, "It's hard to believe that Michael is truly out of our lives for good."

"I know," Ross agreed. "This may sound awful, but I'm grateful."

"Me, too. And that's a sad thing to have to say about someone, but he's been such a dark cloud over us for so long.

At one time, he had so much potential. It makes me wonder just what caused him to go so wrong."

"Did you ever know much about his past?" Ross asked.

"No, not really. He never talked about it. And if he had, I wonder how much of it would have been the truth."

They were nearing Serenity and the closer they got, the safer Maggie felt. A few minutes later they turned onto their gravel road and started up the winding path to their home. Midway through the drive there were cars parked along both sides of the road continuing into the clearing.

As they reached the top of the incline, they heard tumultuous cheering. The yard was filled with men, women and children. It was illuminated by hundreds of candles their friends held high in the air. It looked like half the town of Serenity had turned out to welcome them home. There were yellow ribbons tied to trees and smiling faces everywhere. Caroline, Charlie, Lil, Doc, Kathryn and Mildred were at the front of the crowd. Lindsay was noticeably absent. Maggie determined to find out why tomorrow. For tonight, they would thank the dear, caring people who had come to greet them. Then they would get some much needed rest.

Much later, Maggie and Ross and the children climbed into Maggie and Ross's king size bed to fall asleep. Tonight was a night they all needed to be together. The next morning, Maggie and Ross agreed that it was the most comforting night's sleep they could remember in ages.

CHAPTER 45

Caroline and Charlie visited them the day after Maggie and the children returned home. They were overjoyed to be together again. Both looked haggard, as if they hadn't had much rest. They assured Maggie that would change now that she and their 'grandchildren' were safe. Charlie was managing well on his crutches.

"I don't know how to thank you for coming out to check on us, Charlie," Maggie said. "If you hadn't been so prompt, who knows what would have happened. You saved us valuable time. But I feel just awful that you were hurt in the process."

"A small price to pay for your lives," Charlie said as he embraced Maggie. "We couldn't do without you in our lives."

"After I talked with you yesterday, I called Lindsay," Maggie said. "I didn't get an answer. She didn't come last night either. Is something wrong?"

Caroline and Charlie exchanged glances, then Caroline said, "We didn't want to tell you until you'd had a night's rest, but…"

Maggie was alarmed. "What is it? Is she okay?"

"She is," Caroline said. "She's home resting today. When she got back from bringing Ross dinner and learning that Tom was really Michael, she was awfully upset. And she said she felt guilty. That she had unwittingly helped Michael; she was pretty hard on herself. We tried to tell her she had no way of knowing, even asked her to spend the night in our guest room, but she wouldn't do it. The next morning she woke with terrible cramps. She called Doc. To make a long story short, she lost the baby."

"Oh that's terrible. It breaks my heart." Maggie said. "I have to let her know that we don't blame her for anything Michael did. I feel so sad for her."

"Like I said," Caroline repeated. "She's home resting today. Doc put her on an anti-depressant."

"I need to stop in and talk with her," Maggie said. "Thanks for telling me."

...

A little over a week had passed since the rescue. The children were sleeping in their own beds for part of the night now. They would fall asleep with their parents; then Maggie and Ross would carry them to their own rooms so they could wake up in their own beds and see that they were safe.

Life was slowly returning to normal except that Ross went to the pharmacy late and came home early every day. He was thankful that he had hired Ryan full time two years ago and had recently taken on another pharmacist, Debbie. It allowed him the freedom to be away from his work, the freedom that had become even more important to him recently.

The newspapers had covered the rescue with two huge columns on two different days. The nursing home scandal continued to grow as more evidence from autopsies became public. All of the bodies contained large amounts of Potassium Chloride. With Michael dead, the focus centered on Daniel and Evelyn Anderson. It looked like they wouldn't be seeing one another for years to come, if ever again.

...

The family party with a special surprise for Keri was planned for Saturday evening. She got to choose the dinner menu.

"I want macaroni and cheese, and so does Tyler," she told Maggie. "Isn't that right, Tyler?"

He clapped his hands, gave a little jump and shouted, "Yes!"

Keri continued, "And we want grilled cheese sandwiches and ice cream and chocolate cupcakes, too."

"That sounds wonderful," Maggie said with a chuckle.

"I agree," Ross chimed in.

Maggie went to town on Friday to see Doc. Afterward; she shopped for party hats, balloons and noise makers for their celebration.

Ross came home early, and the whole family worked together on preparing the meal. Keri buttered the bread for the grilled cheese, Ross sliced the cheese, and he and Tyler arranged it on the bread while Maggie stirred the macaroni and cheese and put it in a casserole dish and placed it in the oven.

She and the children had baked cupcakes earlier in the day and put them aside to cool. While Maggie set the dining room table, Ross and Keri frosted the cupcakes and Tyler decorated them with sprinkles. By the time he finished, there were as many sprinkles on the table as on the cupcakes, but no one minded. Then while Maggie kept an eye on the sandwiches in the frying pan and removed the macaroni from the oven and carried it in to the server, Ross blew up the balloons. Everyone was into the party and having a great time, perhaps Maggie most of all.

The children were so excited that they didn't eat very well. It was no surprise to Maggie, but it didn't bother her. She was pleased they were so happy and having such a wonderful time.

Finally dessert was served. That was the only thing that Tyler and Keri ate all of. Then the moment arrived. Maggie had bought gifts for each child to give one another. For Keri, she had a beautiful baby doll that Keri had looked at longingly a few weeks earlier. That was a gift from Tyler. For Tyler, she had found a smaller version of his favorite, current, stuffed animal, Puppy, for Keri to give him.

The gifts were opened with much giggling and squealing. Then they were named, "Lucy" for the doll and "Baby Puppy" for the dog. After that, Maggie began. "This night is so special to us because we have received wonderful news for you, Keri, from your mommy."

"From Mommy? What?"

"When she had to leave you because she was so sick, she wanted you to have a family of your very own here on earth while she watched down on you from heaven. Even though we have loved you from the day you came to stay with us, you weren't really ours yet. But last week, Ross heard from a lawyer. Your mommy told the lawyer that she wanted us to be your adopted mommy and daddy. A mommy and daddy that no one could ever take you away from. When they called Ross, they told us that you are officially our little girl. And we are so happy!"

Keri ran to Maggie. She hugged and kissed her. "I love you so much!" Keri told her. She ran to Ross and did the same, then to Tyler.

Maggie said, "Tyler, do you know what that means?"

He looked at her quizzically.

"It means that now Keri is really your sister!"

"I love you, too," Tyler said to Keri. Then a little giggle escaped his lips. "Forever and ever?"

"Forever and ever and ever," Keri said. "It touched Maggie to hear her say it, as that was what she and her mother had always said to one another."

...

When the party ended Ross and Maggie took the children upstairs. Tyler went to sleep first, and Maggie went back downstairs while Ross finished reading to Keri.

When he joined her in the dining room, Maggie had lit the candles and poured a glass of wine for him.

"Where's yours?" He asked.

"I won't be having any for a while, darling."

"Oh?" He smiled at her.

"Remember how, when you asked me to marry you, you said, 'this is a big house with lots of rooms, and I want to fill it with our children?'"

"Yes." His smile broadened.

"I'm pregnant, Ross."

"We're having a baby? Oh, Maggie, I couldn't be happier." He was at her side instantly.

She rose and he took her in his arms and kissed her deeply. When she came up for air, she said. "This house is going to fill up a little faster than we thought."

He stepped back and looked into her eyes.

"We're finally having one of our own. Doc confirmed it yesterday."

Ross pulled her into another embrace so tightly that she had to pull away to catch her breath.

"The more the merrier, Darling. The more the merrier! I guess we'll be having another big announcement celebration in few weeks. Do you know how much I love you, Maggie?"

"I think I do, Ross. The same way I love you. Forever and beyond." It was the inscription in her wedding band.

"I love you twice forever and beyond. I think that would be infinity," Ross said. He sealed it with another kiss.

EPILOGUE

After several delays the trial for the Andersons began. It had to be moved to another county in order to seat an impartial jury. It lasted for several months. When the verdict finally came in, both were found guilty on six counts of being accomplices to premeditated murder. They were sentenced to forty years each in a maximum security prison.

Charlie's injuries healed, and he and Caroline continued to dote on Maggie, Ross and the children. They eagerly awaited the birth of the baby.

Lil and the widower, David Helms, continued their friendship. They were seen together socially quite often even sitting together in church on Sundays. Everyone began to think the town "match-maker" had met her match.

Lindsay had a difficult time shaking her guilt for the unwitting part she played in the abduction of Maggie and the children. Maggie continued to be unwaivering, constantly assuring Lindsay that she held her in no way responsible. Michael had duped yet another trusting soul. In time, Lindsay forgave herself. She was slowly recovering from the depression of losing her unborn child. And there was a new interest in her life.

When Adam Cassidy opened his accounting office in Serenity, Doc was happy to switch his accounts over to him. He preferred to do business locally but had no one to deal with in Serenity until Adam came to town. Doc put Lindsay in charge of co-coordinating with Adam on the clinic's business. Before long, Lindsay and Adam became friends. Soon after, they began to date. All of their friends were pleased and hopeful for them. Lil couldn't have been happier.

Kevin and Carlie were married in June. Lil was thrilled. She was in her glory as she helped plan the wedding. Kevin asked Ross to be one of his ushers and Maggie was in charge of the guest book. Tyler was the ring bearer and Keri made an adorable flower girl.

In late November, Maggie gave birth to fraternal twins. She and Ross named them Judith and James, for Maggie's late mother and father. The whole family, including Caroline and Charlie, waited at the hospital to greet the newest little Harringtons.

~~The End~~

...

A New Beginning

Return to Serenity

Dixie Land

To request more copies of following books by Dixie Land, please use the order form below or contact the author at ljdixie@aol.com

        Return to Serenity____ $15.00
        Second Chances_____ $15.00
        Promises to Keep_____ $15.00
        Circle of secrets_____ $15.00
        Exit Wounds_____ $15.00
        Serenity_____ $15.00
        Finding Faith_____ $15.00

Please send me _____ copy/copies of Return to Serenity
Please send me _____ copy/copies of Second Chances
Please send me _____ copy/copies of Promises to Keep
Please send me _____ copy/copies of Circle of Secrets
Please send me _____ copy/copies of Exit Wounds
Please send me _____ copy/copies of Serenity
Please send me _____ copy/copies of Finding Faith

I am enclosing $_____ (please add $2.50 for shipping/handling for the first book and .50 for each additional book.)

Book Total $ _____
Postage and handling $ _____
Total Amount Due $ _____

Please mail this form with your check or money order
(no cash or C.O.D.'s) to
Dixie Land
Alabaster Book Publishing
P.O. Box 401
Kernersville, NC 27285
www.heartofdixiebooks.com
www.publisheralabaster.biz

_____

Address:_____

_____State:_____

Printed in the United States
75936LV00005B/61-192